Wanted: Bookkeeper

Sophie Dawson

Stories in Faithful Living

Copyright © 2018 Sophie Dawson

All rights reserved.

ISBN: 978-1-63376-035-6

No part of this publication maybe reproduced or distributed in print or electronic form without prior permission of the author. Please respect the hard work of the author and do not participate in or encourage the piracy of copyrighted materials.

This is a work of fiction. The people, unless you recognize the name of a real historical person, are not real. They, too, have been created by me, my friend and author George McVey, or the other authors of the Silverpines Series. This is true of Nugget Nate and Penny Ryder and Nathan Ryder, who may or may not show up in this book. Even if real historical people are mentioned their lives may or may not adhere strictly to documented historical reference. In other words, what they do or say has little bearing in fact and they probably didn't do or say it. This is a fictional story after all.

DEDICATION

As odd as it seems, this book is dedicated to my cat, Snookers. He's been my companion for 21 years sitting beside me, or on me, or near me all my years of professional quilting and writing. He's showing his age and most likely won't be around much longer. He's a sweet cat who loves me as much as I do him.

DESCRIPTION

Tilde Lasek needs a husband. Running the family bank after the disaster that killed most of the men of Silverpines, Oregon, including her father and brother, is simply too hard. She doesn't have enough banking knowledge to be successful. Against her mother's wishes, Tilde places an advertisement in the Groom's Gazette. She's smart enough to know not to ask for a banker. Instead she asks for a bookkeeper.

Joel Richards, dissatisfied living in his hometown after he's betrayed by his fiancé, answers the advertisement and soon is heading west. He knows his banking experience will be helpful in whatever business he'll be bookkeeper for. Besides, Tilde is beautiful. His new mother-in-law isn't happy with the marriage. Then there are the changes Joel hopes to make at the bank. Tilde's not happy with them.

Can Joel convince Tilde to bring Silverpines bank into the 20th century? Will Tilde be able to be the wife he wants without letting him bring even more change to her life? Will Mabel Lasek ever accept her daughter's marriage? Will there be a Happily Ever After with all three living in the same house?

CHAPTER ONE

SILVERPINES, OREGON
July 7, 1899

Flopping down in the middle of the parlor settee, Tilde Lasek spread her legs out straight in a quite unladylike manner. If her mother saw her position there would be a severe look and very possibly a critical comment. Right now Tilde didn't care. She'd just gone through a traumatic event and was going to do something she knew her mother wouldn't like, but Tilde decided it was necessary. It was what she'd wanted to do back in May when the other women placed their advertisements in the Groom's Gazette, but her mother had fiercely objected.

In April the town of Silverpines, Oregon had suffered two earthquakes which destroyed the silver mine and Timber Town logging camp. This resulted in the deaths of most of the men. Tilde's father and brother had perished in the second quake trying to rescue those trapped in the mine. The mine collapsed on the miners as well as those attempting to save them.

Without their husbands, fathers, brothers, and acceptable suitors the women were left running businesses and picking up the pieces of their lives. The struggle to learn how to run the businesses, as well as conmen and outlaws coming to town, brought the young women to Betsy Sewell who had advertised for her new husband, marrying him in March. Alexzander Sewell was now the town sheriff and they were expecting their first baby in February.

Tilde and her mother had argued for nearly a week about placing an advertisement until Tilde let the matter drop. Today, however, made her determined to do so no matter what her mother said.

Tilde closed her eyes and sighed, the events of the day replayed in her mind. She'd been working at the desk behind the teller windows. The bank door opened and three men with bandanas covering the bottom half of their faces ran in.

"Well, what have we here?" The man with a red bandana asked, his eyes bright with evil intent. "I do believe it's the lovely Tilde Lasek. You just open all the cash drawers and step right out here." He waved a pistol in the direction of the gate to the counter. The other two pulled their six-shooters out too.

Her hands trembling, she did as told. The two outlaws came and began taking cash, putting it in a grimy canvas bag. As soon as Tilde passed through the gate the man holding the gun on her grabbed her arm, pulling her to him. He holstered his six-gun and pulled down his bandana.

"I'm gonna take me a little bit o' sugar. If it tastes good, I just might take me more than the money."

Tilde struggled to keep his lips from pressing against hers.

The door burst open, slamming against the wall.

"Stop, you're under arrest. Let go of Miss Lasek," Marshal Sewell yelled as he ran in. With him were Clay Cutler, new husband to Millie Messer, owner of the mercantile, and Mason Dekum who had married Sarah Gillham, daughter of the gun shop owner who'd perished in the disaster.

It was all over in a few minutes. They'd been the longest few minutes in Tilde's life. It also cemented her conviction that she needed a husband to help run the bank. The outlaws were taken to jail and Tilde closed the bank for the day and was escorted home.

"Tilde, what are you doing home this time of day? And please reposition yourself as a lady should sit."

Tilde opened one eye to see her mother standing in the arched doorway leading from the sitting room to the parlor. Pulling her feet back, she sat up. The glare didn't leave her mother's face.

"Well?" Mabel Lasek tapped her foot impatiently. "Why are you not at the bank?"

"I'm taking the rest of the day off. I don't care that it's

closed. I don't need masses of people coming in asking about what happened." Tilde blew out a breath with a puff. Another unladylike action.

"So, are you going to tell me what happened?" Now Mabel's hands were fisted on her hips.

"Three men came into the bank to rob it. They threatened to take me with them when they left. Sheriff Sewell, Clay Cutler, and Mason Dekum came in and stopped them. I haven't a clue how they knew the bank was being robbed but I'm thankful they did."

Mabel's hands flew to her mouth. She ran across the room, sitting down beside her daughter. "Are you all right? They didn't hurt you, did they?" Her hands fluttered around Tilde as if checking for injury.

"I'm fine. At least physically. It was a terrifying time. That's why I closed the bank. There is no way I could keep working. It's difficult enough on a regular day." She raised a shaking hand and tucked a lock of hair behind her ear. Who knew what her coiffure looked like now.

"Oh, my baby. What an awful thing to have happened." Mabel put her arm around Tilde, pulling her against her. Tilde couldn't hold the tears back any longer. They'd been threatening since the robbery attempt. Safe in her mother's arms, she sobbed out her fear and relief while her back was lovingly rubbed.

When the tears were spent, Mabel helped her now exhausted daughter up the stairs, into a nightgown, and tucked her into bed. Tilde lay there forming the advertisement in her mind until she fell asleep.

~~~~~

August 1899

Joel Richards leaned back in his desk chair. No one was in the Cottonwood State Bank at the moment and he was caught up with his work. Sure there were things he could do, but resting a few minutes from calculations would refresh his mind. The newspaper his boss, Eustace Taylor, put on his desk after he'd finished it tempted him. Knowing Eustace wouldn't mind if he read it, Joel picked it up. As he opened it a flyer fell out onto the floor. The headline was 'Groom's Gazette.' Joel grinned as he grabbed it from the floor. The flyer held advertisements for mail order brides for men out west. Though the peak of seeking women to move west was past, there were enough advertisements to keep the publication going.

Joel scanned the notices. One man wanted a redhead with blue eyes to come to Colorado. Another didn't care what she looked like as long as she could cook. He sat up when he saw one different from all the others.

'Wanted: Bookkeeper to move to Silverpines, Oregon to marry a young woman needing help running a successful business.'

There was a post office box in Maine as the address. If interested, the man would include the number contained in the advertisement when he answered it.

Staring at the ad, Joel tried to push down the

excitement filling him. Maybe this was what he needed. A total change of his life.

The past year had been filled with highs and lows he hadn't experienced since he was nearly three, when his mother died giving birth to his sister, Anne. She had nearly starved to death when she couldn't take cow or goat milk. Another tragedy led Katie Reed to nurse Anne, take care of Joel, and run the house for his father, Sheriff Drew Richards. From that low came a marriage of convenience between them that became one of love. Four more children were born into the family.

The high for Joel this year had been the 'yes' Constance Bishop gave him when he proposed. They were planning their June wedding when he found her kissing Clem Diller whose hands were touching places on Constance only her husband should. The betrothal was broken with many tears and promises from her, but Joel wasn't interested in a woman who didn't hold her promise to love only him.

That low led to his present dissatisfaction with life. Joel knew he had much to be thankful for. His parents and siblings were happy and healthy. Anne was married to her high school sweetheart and expecting their first child. His other siblings were still in school busy with studies, activities, and the general horsing around of teenagers.

His job as assistant manager of Cottonwood State Bank was not as lofty as it sounded. He did whatever Mr. Taylor didn't want to do. Joel was getting a good overview of what running a bank entailed, but he didn't think there was much of a possibility for advancement. Eustace was healthy and vigorous, not intending to retire any time soon. Even then, Joel doubted he'd advance to the president's position or pay scale.

Joel read the advertisement again.

The bank's door opened.

"Eustace, Eustace, are you here? You'll never believe what I just saw." Mrs. Beulah Taylor's loud shrill nearly made Joel wince. As much as he loved the banker's wife as a surrogate grandmother, her voice and nosey attitude wearied him.

He looked up and his eyes widened just a bit. One would think she'd get tired of wearing such a color combination. Fuchsia and chartreuse. All through his growing up years Grambo, as Cottonwood's children called her, had at least one garment in those colors. Each new one became a topic of conversation.

"Oh, hello, Mr. Richards. It always seems odd to call you that. I remember when you were just a small boy. We had our moments, for sure. You've grown into such a handsome man. I don't know what Constance Bishop was thinking when she threw you over for that no 'count Clem Diller. I'm sure you are better off without her.

"Is my husband in his office?" She fluttered her hands, touching the fuchsia feather on her chartreuse hat. Joel had to admit she was still a good-looking woman. Too bad she didn't know how to mind her own business.

"I'm sorry, Mrs. Taylor, he went over to City Hall

about half an hour ago. I'm not sure he's coming back before the bank closes."

"Well, bother. I suppose I'll have to wait until he comes home to tell him." She struck a pose Joel knew was meant for him to comment on her outfit.

"Mrs. Taylor, you look striking today, even more so than usual." Her smile and fake humble expression told Joel his comment fulfilled her expectations.

"Well, dear boy, I'll leave you to your work. Don't forget the set up for the Corn Boil and Catfish Fry. It's this Friday."

Joel waved as she looked back, giving her parting instructions. He'd help set up but he most likely wouldn't attend. Constance and Clem would be there. He didn't need his nose rubbed into their affairs.

Putting a sheet of paper in the typewriter, Joel set to work answering the advertisement in the Grooms Gazette.

CHAPTER TWO

SEPTEMBER, 1899

Joel turned from gazing out the window of the Pullman car down to the letter held in his hand. There was no need to read it because he knew it by heart. Her name was Tilde Lasek. She was twenty years old. Her father and brother were both killed in the disaster that happened to Silverpines in April. She lived with her mother and they owned a successful business. Tilde was running the business but needed help for it to continue prospering.

Seems that a number of young women and widows had advertised for husbands earlier and they seemed to be making their marriages work. Tilde didn't say why she hadn't advertised before.

She described herself as not overly tall but not short. A little skinnier than she'd like. Eyes too large for her face and ordinary light brown hair. Oh, her eyes were green.

They had exchanged several letters before she wrote that, if he were willing, she was ready to throw caution to the wind and marry him.

What struck Joel as odd is that she never said what the business was that her mother now owned. Mabel Lasek didn't work there, so all the responsibility now fell on Tilde's shoulders. He'd told her of his banking background and asked what his job would entail but her answer was that his qualifications were sufficient for him to do everything required.

Well, he would find out soon. He'd sent a telegram earlier in the day at a stop to let her know he was arriving today and hopefully on time.

Looking out the window again, Joel didn't see the countryside passing. Instead he saw the shock then tears in the eyes of his family when he told them he was leaving Cottonwood, Iowa and heading west to Oregon.

After his siblings were in bed, Joel told them of the advertisement and the letters he and Tilde had sent back and forth. He also told them of his difficulty in seeing Constance and Clem on the street, at church, and at every function held in town. He wanted a new start away from his disappointment in her, and also feeling that he was as high in his position at work as he would ever be.

Though they hated that he was leaving home, his parents understood. They were concerned that by marrying as soon as he arrived, he was looking to be hurt again. Marriage was for life. It could either be wonderful or lead to years of heartache and misery.

Joel's goal was to make it wonderful. He planned to be as devoted a husband as his father was to Katie Mama. He smiled at the memory of the day she was so mad at Drew she'd left the house, leaving Joel and the infant Annie with him. She hadn't even come home to nurse the baby. Pastor Lendrey came to take the baby to her, letting his pa know what he thought of how he'd treated her. As far as Joel knew, his pa never did something that stupid again.

Katie was a wonderful mother, never treating Joel or Annie differently from the way she treated the children born later. Though he now didn't remember the mother who gave him birth, he had sometimes wished he could.

As a three-year-old, Joel was mourning his mother's death. Katie had made a quilt from two of her dresses, adding some other fabrics including a few squares of pink, a color he'd loved at the time. He had forgotten to pack the quilt and bring with him. It was worn, patched in places, and he hated that he had left it behind. It represented two women who had loved him unconditionally.

"Silverpines, next stop. Silverpines, Oregon in fifteen minutes," the conductor called as he walked through the car.

Joel tucked the letter into his inside coat pocket. He'd slept in the upper bunk and packed his satchel in the early morning. Now all he had to do was wait. He focused on the countryside again, wanting to know what the land near Silverpines was like.

The conductor came through again, calling the five-minute warning. Joel stood, grabbed his satchel, and went to the car platform. From there he watched as the town of his future came into sight.

~~~~~

Tilde locked the bank after placing the 'back in thirty minutes' sign in the window. She pulled the net veil of her hat down under her chin and smoothed her skirt as she walked to the train station. Her dress was not her best, as her mother would have questioned why she was wearing it to work in the bank. Still, it was one of her newer ones.

The rust and tan plaid with green trim went well with her hair. At least she thought so. Tilde was glad the style of sleeves was narrower than it had been a few years back. She'd loved the huge puffed sleeves when they first came into fashion. Having to wear steel hoop sleeve supports dimmed her preference for the style. They also wouldn't have been comfortable to work in at the bank.

She did love the wideness of the skirt. It showed off her narrow waist, which she was proud didn't need a tightly laced corset. It wasn't right to be proud of that, but she was anyway.

The day was cool with big fluffy clouds in the September sky. With a furtive glance around, Tilde was pleased not to see anyone on the street near the station. She really didn't want anyone to be asking what she was doing. No one knew she was expecting a man to arrive.

A man who would be her husband in the very near future. Especially, she didn't want her mother to find out.

Tilde hadn't told her mother about the advertisement or the responses she'd received. They'd all come to her at the post office box of the bank.

She'd been surprised at the number of inquiries. Many she threw in the trash bin as soon as she read them. Then, she'd sorted the ones that had potential. She'd responded to three, making inquiries as to their qualifications as bookkeepers, as well as personal priorities and life goals. The one from Joel Richards stood out in several ways.

That he worked at a bank pushed his to the top. That he wrote of his commitment to his faith also set his apart from most of the others. His goals were to be a competent employee, a caring husband, and Godly father.

He sounded too good to be true. He must have thought it sounded the same as he'd added several incidents from his growing up years illustrating some of his faults. He'd stated he hoped he'd grown out of that behavior but couldn't guarantee it. That had made her laugh.

Joel, as she'd begun to think of him instead of Mr. Richards, not pressing her for the details of what the business he'd be working in when she evaded his question also impressed her. Many of the men had started their letters with inquiries about it.

The whistle announcing the approaching train broke

into her thoughts as she stood under the awning of the station. Tilde hoped no one she knew would be coming to board the train or disembarking. It wasn't that she was ashamed or wanted to keep her coming marriage a secret. It was just that she wanted to keep it from her mother until she spoke with Joel and they made plans, and he understood what the situation was.

Another whistle and a whoosh of steam brought the train to a stop. Jackson Hershall, a thirteen-year-old orphan who did odd jobs around town, crossed the platform to the baggage car. He would unload whatever was to remain in Silverpines. Tilde trusted Jackson to keep his tongue between his teeth about her meeting a man, especially as she planned to slip some coins into his hand.

A movement at the platform of the car brought her attention back to watch for the man she planned to marry. The thought brought the butterflies in her stomach to life. She pressed her hands against it. It was as if there were a million in there all trying to break out. In her gloves, Tilde's hands sweated more than the warmth of the day warranted.

Standing there was a lean, tall man wearing a gray travel suit with a wide brimmed gray hat. He had a modest mustache and short beard that appeared black or dark brown. He scanned the platform of the station until he saw her standing in the shade. One side of his mouth quirked up and he stepped down.

Tilde suddenly had no clue how one met their

unknown future husband. What did one say? Should she shake his hand? Her fingers clenched together. She was frozen to the spot, unable to lift her feet to move. It didn't make any difference as he was walking straight to her.

"Don't be afraid. I don't bite. At least not since I was five. I bit my sister Annie and received a spanking and lecture I still remember." Joel grinned at her and held out his hand. "Joel Richards. I assume you are Miss Tilde Lasek."

"Y…yes, I am. Pl…pleased to meet you, Mr. Richards." Tilde lifted her hand and her weak grip was shaken by a firm one.

Joel looked around, seeing Jackson loading two trunks onto a dolly. "Where shall I direct my baggage to be taken?"

"Um, the Silverpines Inn. Jackson probably knows that but here, take this and ask him to please not spread your arrival around." Tilde held out her coins. Joel lifted an eyebrow, ignored the coins, and carried his satchel across to the young man. As he chatted with Jackson, who took the satchel, Tilde saw him pull coins from his pocket and give them to the teen.

When Joel returned, he held out his arm. "May I escort you to wherever we are to become more familiar with each other?"

Heat flushed Tilde's face. Becoming more familiar was a fascinating idea, especially since they planned to marry. They would be much more familiar with each other very soon. An intriguing feeling passed through her as she took his arm and turned, walking to the steps leading down to the street.

CHAPTER THREE

THE STREET THEY CROSSED WAS dirt and rutted. So different from the cobbled streets of Cottonwood. Joel walked beside Tilde until she reached the steps up to the boardwalk in front of a building, then he paused to allow her to proceed him. He thought she would walk along but was surprised when she stopped at the first building and put a key into the lock. He looked up and his mouth dropped.

"This is your business?"

"Yes, come in. I'm not wanting to have this conversation on the street."

Tilde pushed the door open and went in. Joel followed. The bank itself was not large: Two teller windows with a desk behind the black granite counter. A couple of straight chairs under the front window. She went past the desk and into a room near the back. Joel wiped his fingers down his mustache. Never had he thought the business she ran would be a bank.

He found her removing her hat, placing it and the pin that held it in place on a small shelf in the corner. She turned and looked at him.

"Please, have a seat. We can chat here. I can tend to any customers who might come in." Tilde sat in the large swivel office chair behind the broad mahogany desk. She looked like a child sitting in her father's chair. She was, the thought came to him. Not a child. No, her curves showed she was a woman. But she was petite in bone structure and thin, as she'd said in her letter. It was her green eyes that gave the illusion. Large and open, framed with long lashes. They gave her the look of youth and innocence. Which is exactly what she was.

Joel knew she was twenty, barely. She'd written that her birthday was July 14th. It was mid-September now. It suddenly struck him how short a time had elapsed between when he first saw the advertisement and today. Nine weeks, maybe ten. Not a lot of time to make such a life changing decision.

Tilde cleared her throat. Her gloves now rested on the desk. She was fiddling with the fingers. Her nervousness was palpable and the desire to give her a hug of comfort almost had him rising from his seat.

"Mr. Richards…"

"Please, call me Joel. If we are going to marry, I think we can be a bit more intimate."

As she blushed and dropped her eyes, he knew his phrasing didn't relieve her of her tension. In fact, they may have added a new layer.

"Yes, um, Joel. Please call me Tilde."

When she didn't continue, Joel decided to begin the conversation. "I understand why you didn't tell what your business was. A wise choice."

"Thank you. I didn't want to advertise for a banker. I would have had all sorts of conmen writing me. There were enough of those anyway."

When Tilde didn't continue, Joel did. "You wrote me about the earthquakes and deaths of your father and brother. Please accept my sympathies. I know I wrote them to you, but I wanted to tell you in person."

"Thank you." Tears filled Tilde's eyes. "It's been difficult. Everything was happening so fast. The mine collapse, mudslide, all the deaths, then trying to pick up the pieces of our lives. The conmen and outlaws coming to town. Trying to keep the bank working.

"So many families leaving town, abandoning their houses and mortgages. Mother refusing to help. I was simply a teller before. I didn't know how to do so many of the banking procedures. Trying to learn them with no one to teach me and no books to read. Then the attempted robbery." The words came tumbling over each other.

When Joel saw Tilde brush tears from her face, he couldn't stop himself. He stood and went around the desk. Lifting her from the chair, he pulled her to his chest, his arms wrapping around her, stroking his hand up and down her back.

"You never had a chance to grieve, did you? You can

now. I'm here and can take some of the burden off of you."

When Tilde broke down sobbing, he knew he'd said the right thing. Offered the comfort and support she needed. He marveled at how right she felt in his arms. Lifting her slightly, Joel turned and sat in the chair with her on his lap. He didn't care that it wasn't proper. Didn't care that if someone saw it would cause a scandal. They were to be married, after all.

All doubt he'd had before meeting her vanished. Coming here was right. Joel had prayed hard before he sent the first letter. He prayed each day asking for guidance. When everything preceded so smoothly, he knew this was God's will.

Even then he doubted. Was he really following what God wanted him to do? Was he mistaken? The questions had rolled around in his mind even on the train trip west. Especially on the train. Now, they were ashes in the wind. Blown away by the feel of her in his arms and the sound of her sobs.

~~~~~

As her grief drained away with her tears, Tilde became aware of where she was and with whom. She jerked upright, away from his chest. When she tried to stand, his arms held her in place.

"Just relax and catch your breath. Are you feeling better?" Joel's hand resumed the stroking of her back.

Tilde took several deep breaths. A thought of their conversation brought a giggle to her lips. "Is this the 'bit more intimate' you were expecting?"

A twinkle came into his eyes and he gave her a mischievous grin. "Not quite so soon, but it seemed appropriate for the circumstances. I hope there will be more moments of intimacy after we marry."

Tilde felt herself blush from her head to her toes. She'd thought about the physical aspects of marriage. Aspects she wasn't supposed to know about. Her mother certainly hadn't mentioned them. Her good friend, Sarah, gave her a general description after she married Mason Dekum.

"Are you feeling better, Tilde?" The concern in Joel's eyes eased her blush.

"Yes, I'm sorry I blubbered all over you."

"Had you expressed your grief at all since everything happened?"

"Not really. We had a mass service for all those who died. It didn't seem real at the time. Nothing was personal. It couldn't be. There were just too many being honored. Mother went into seclusion for a few weeks. I had to run the bank. It was a busy time and I only hope I did everything correctly."

"I'm sure you did your best. We'll sort it out. How is your mother now?"

Tilde gave a frustrated sigh. "That's something we will need to talk about." She stood up. "I'm going to go freshen up. I won't be long."

When she returned, Joel was standing, looking out the window. She knew he could see the railroad tracks, depot, jail, the house where Sheriff Sewell and Betsy lived, as well as the docks along the river. He turned and smiled at her.

"Welcome back. You look refreshed."

"Thank you." She quirked her lips to the side. "Now, I need to prepare you for my mother. Have a seat. This will take a while and we need to decide how to proceed."

Joel shot her a quizzical look that she waved away as she sat in front of the desk, allowing him to sit behind it.

"Is your mother a formidable person?" Joel placed his elbows on the desk and steepled his fingers.

"She loves me but to me she is. A better word might be intractable. She has very firm opinions and is quite forceful in making them known.

"She would not, in any way, 'entertain the thought of working at the bank. I have never worked outside my home a day in my life and I will not lower myself to do so now.'" Tilde's voice took on an imperious tone.

"Ouch, what an insult to you."

"She doesn't see it that way. That really isn't the issue. She wouldn't be an asset here. She has no head for numbers. Father used to say she couldn't count to twenty if her shoes were on."

They laughed. It felt good to remember her father and laugh. There hadn't been much to laugh about since the disaster.

"With so many young women now running the

businesses, conmen and outlaws came to town. Sheriff Sewell and his deputies have done the best they could. Many have been captured, but that's not where I wanted to go with this.

"We young ladies and the young widows in town realized the need for men to marry and help with running those businesses. We went to Betsy Sewell because she'd advertised in the Groom's Gazette and brought Alexzander Sewell to town. She gave us the information so we could submit ads. She's another good friend.

"When I told my mother, she threw a hissy fit. A huge hissy fit, the likes of which I'd never seen before and I've seen them my whole life.

"I decided right then wasn't the time for me to place an ad. I honored my mother and set the information aside. I prayed that if God wanted me to send for a husband, He would give me a sign that I'd know the time was right. If I didn't get the sign, well, I wasn't supposed to place an ad.

"The attempted bank robbery was my sign. I realized how vulnerable I was alone here in the bank. There was no way I could stop them from doing what they wanted. And they wanted more than the money."

Tilde looked down and swallowed the fear that rose every time she thought of the man holding and trying to kiss her. She didn't even want to think about what could have happened if the sheriff and his men hadn't come in.

"That's when I knew it was time." She hated the tremor in her voice. "I wrote the advertisement that night."

"I'm sorry you had to go through that. How did your mother take the news?" Joel leaned back in the chair.

"That's just it. I haven't told her." Tilde bit her lip.

~~~~~

Joel lifted an eyebrow. "So, she doesn't know about me coming and us marrying."

"No."

Joel rubbed a hand down his face. This was lovely. Here he was in a new town, planning on marrying Tilde, and her mother doesn't know and was against the idea in the first place.

Beulah Taylor's image flashed through his mind. Seems he'd left one bossy, determined woman and found another one. And she was going to be his mother-in-law.

"So, how do you want to proceed? Are we going to get married and present a fait accompli? Or shall we invite her to our wedding?"

Tilde's wide eyes got wider. "I don't know. I never went past you arriving in my thoughts. What do you think?"

"Since I've never met the woman it's difficult for me to say which will be the least traumatic to her."

Joel watched as Tilde worked the problem out in her mind. So many expressions and emotions crossed her face in such a short time he was caught between laughing at the sight and comforting her again for her distress.

She seemed to come to a conclusion when she straightened her spine. "I think it will be best to present the fait accompli. We will be legally married. I'm of age so there's no problem there. The most she can do is have a hissy fit, right?" It seemed as if she shrunk down a little as if not to be seen.

"She could bar me from the bank. Then you wouldn't have the help you need."

"Then she will have to run it herself because I'll quit." Though the words were bold, Tilde hunched down a little more. It was clear she was expecting trouble from her mother and wasn't looking forward to it.

"Let's hope it doesn't go that far."

CHAPTER FOUR

"HAVE A GOOD DAY, MR. Cutler."

"You too, Miss Lasek."

Joel heard Tilde lock the door. The afternoon had been slow and Joel had stayed out of sight in the office as they discussed her decision to marry before they told her mother. He had gone to check into the inn earlier, making sure he got the best room. His trunks had been delivered from the station and would be taken up. He went to stand in the office doorway and saw her pull the cash drawer out. He stepped back as she brought it to the office.

"As soon as I balance the drawer and close the safe we can go to the parsonage. Abby, Pastor James' wife, will be there and can be a witness for us. She placed an ad for a husband too. She's a friend and will understand why I want to marry before telling Mother."

"You're sure you want to do this today? We can wait until tomorrow or even later. I can stay at the inn until then."

Tilde laid the bills she'd counted back in the drawer. "I don't think that's a good plan. When word of you coming to town gets around, and it will, people will wonder why; and unless you are planning to hide in your room, they will ask you and then either you'll have to lie or we risk Mother finding out and stopping us. We need to tie the knot today."

Joel cleared his throat. "Um, what about tonight? Also, where are we going to live?"

Tilde's face turned red. Nervous sweat beaded on her forehead. She pulled the handkerchief tucked in her sleeve out and blotted it away.

Joel's eyebrow lifted and his lips twitched, trying to hide a grin. "Another thing you didn't think about?"

"No." The word was spoken sheepishly as she looked at the floor.

Moving to stand behind her, Joel laid his hands on her shoulders. It was a bold move but if they were to marry, they were going to be touching each other. Tilde took a sharp intake of breath.

"It will be okay. Even though we will marry today, there won't be anything else until we are ready. We do need to talk about where we will begin our married life though."

"I know. It's just, I never planned for it."

Joel leaned forward and whispered in her ear. "A little shortsighted, huh?"

A shudder ran through her. "Yes. Let me put this in

the safe and lock it." She stepped away from him and rounded the desk with the drawer in her hands.

Joel followed her to the safe and watched her as she locked it. He'd need to learn the combination, but that could wait. The banking wasn't the priority. Tilde and he getting married was.

Tilde turned around and studied him. "What would you think about living at my house with my mother? It might help her get to know you and not feel so abandoned."

Joel wasn't sure about how that would work. "I'm willing to give it a try. But I want us to spend the night at the inn. We may not do anything, but I don't think we want your mother listening in the hall."

"Oh my, no. Besides, she's going to need some cool down time. We may need to spend several nights at the inn. I'll pay for it."

"No, I'm the groom. This honeymoon is on me."

~~~~~

Tilde's hands shook as she held on to Joel's. They were in the parlor of the parsonage with Mrs. Fannie Pearl Edmondson standing beside her and Abby James next to Joel. They were reciting their vows before Pastor James.

Tilde was nervous for more than one reason. She was marrying a virtual stranger. Pastor James had given them advice on making a marriage of convenience a success which sounded like a lot of work. And the most nerve wrecking of all, she was now very late getting home from work. Her mother would be upset about that without even considering Tilde was bringing home a husband. Well, maybe her nerves about their spending the night together at the inn rivaled that of telling her mother.

Pastor James blessing a ring brought Tilde back into the service. In his hand lay a gold band. She bit her lip. She hadn't thought she'd have a wedding ring. Some women didn't. Joel seemed to be a very thoughtful man. Their discussions at the bank showed that, and now this. She smiled at him as he placed the ring on her finger. The surprise in his eyes that it fit matched hers.

"I now pronounce you husband and wife." Pastor James closed his Bible.

"No kiss?" Joel raised his eyebrow.

"If you want, you certainly may, but with these marriages of strangers it can be uncomfortable."

Once again, Tilde felt the flush of her cheeks. How many times had she blushed today? She couldn't remember, but it was definitely the most she'd ever done in one day. As she thought of the rest of what would happen today she knew there would be many more. Her blush heightened when Joel leaned down and kissed her on the cheek.

"Best wishes, my dear." Mrs. Edmondson drew Tilde into a hug. "If you ever need me, you know where I live." Whispering in Tilde's ear, she said, "He seems to be a very good man. I'll be praying for you both. Especially in how your mother will handle it. I'll come visit her tomorrow. She can rant and rave at me all she wants. It will help her get over her shock."

"Thank you. I know we'll appreciate it."

"No problem, my dear."

"Best wishes, Tilde." Abby pulled her into a tight hug. "I'm so happy for you. I know you wanted this before, but I think God had you wait so you would get this handsome man." She turned to Joel and lifted a finger, shaking it at him. "You be good to her or you'll answer to me, you hear?"

Pastor James pulled his wife back against his chest. "Abby, I know you feel protective, but let the threats wait until they are needed. I don't think they will be." He smiled at Tilde and Joel who stood just behind Tilde's right shoulder.

"Don't you worry, Mrs. James. I know how to treat a lady and my wife is definitely a lady."

Mrs. Edmondson clapped her gloved hands together. "You two had better get on your way. You are way late getting home, Tilde. Your mother will be mad about that on top of you getting married."

"Oh my, yes," Tilde said. "I should have been home at least an hour ago. Supper should nearly be ready." Giving each woman a final hug, and a heartfelt thank-you to Pastor James, Tilde grabbed Joel by the hand and pulled him out the front door.

~~~~~

The parsonage was just a block and a half from the Lasek House. Joel tried to take in the large ornate home. It rivaled any of the most magnificent homes built in

Cottonwood recently.

Set in the center of an entire block the two and a half story house had clay colored siding trimmed in a dark gray. Yellow fish scale decoration banded between the floors of the bay gracing the side of the house. A round turret with large curved windows also had trim of fish scales. A porch wrapped from the bay around and across the front with steps on both sides. Bronze eagles with wings spread decorated each side of the stair borders. Bushes lined the porch.

Tilde pulled him along, across the lawn, and up the side steps onto the porch. Though there was a door just to their left, she rounded the turret heading for the front door. Joel tried to look in the windows as they passed but only caught glimpses of the rooms. Tilde stopped short, right in front of the double doors. There were stained glass panels in each one.

"Okay, I can do this. She can't kill me, and we can always just leave." Tilde looked at him and let out a big breath. "Right? We can just go to the hotel and have supper there if she pitches too much of a fit?"

"Yes, of course." Joel didn't know what to think. This woman sounded worse than Beulah Taylor ever was. What had he gotten himself into?

Tilde straightened her shoulders and took another deep breath. "Okay, I'm ready to beard the dragon." She placed her hand on the door handle.

Joel waited for her to press the latch. And waited. "Tilde?"

"Yes?"

"Are we going in or not?"

"Um, yes?"

"Today?"

"Could we do it tomorrow?" She peeked at him through the veil of her hat.

Joel fought the grin pulling at his lips. She definitely was afraid of her mother. Stepping closer, he lifted the hand he held and kissed the back of her gloved fingers. "I'll be right beside you. If it gets too bad, I'll step in and announce we are leaving and will see her in a few days. I can be pretty formidable when I want to be. My father is the sheriff of Cottonwood so I know how to talk real fierce." He took a stance he'd seen his pa use many times with a commanding expression. It got the response he wanted. She giggled.

"I'm ready now. I think." Tilde pressed the latch and pushed the door open. "Welcome to Lasek House, my home."

The entry was paneled entirely in carved wood, both walls and ceiling. There was a small nook just to the right with a leaded glass window and a hall tree. Next to it was a wide staircase that went up several steps to a landing then turned, proceeding up along the exterior wall, turned again causing a slanted ceiling in the entry. A marble topped table sat below the slant. Tilde was unpinning her hat. Her gloves now lay on the table.

"Tilde, is that you? Why are you so late? Dara nearly has supper ready. It was very ill-mannered of you not to let us know you would be late." A woman, who must be Tilde's mother approached from the back of the house.

"I'm sorry, Mother." Tilde set her hat down and took hold of Joel's hand. "Mother, I'd like you to meet Mr. Joel Richards, my husband." The last two words were nearly whispered.

"What?" The shriek hurt Joel's ears. "Tilde Adelaide Lasek, what do you mean your husband?" Mrs. Lasek began fanning herself with her hand.

"Let's move to the parlor. We can sit and tell you everything." Tilde looked at Joel, her eyes pleading.

He nodded, but not knowing where the parlor was he had to wait for one of the ladies to show him the way. It wasn't a long wait. Mrs. Lasek turned on her heel, pushed a set of doors open, and marched into the room.

It was the room with the bay of three windows with stained glass headers and a door to the porch. The wood ceiling was simpler with small beams running one direction and larger ones the other. Cream walls with wood wainscoting that held paintings were highlighted by a black marble fireplace. Several seating groups of furniture made cozy conversation spots, upholstered in cream and blue stripes. He and Tilde settled on the settee with Mrs. Lasek on a wing backed chair.

"So, what's this about you being my daughter's husband and why didn't I know about this?" Mrs. Lasek first stabbed Joel with a fierce look, then Tilde.

"Mother, you know I wanted to advertise for a husband back in May when the other ladies were writing. You didn't want me to, so I honored your desire. It's been very difficult for me to run the bank. I don't know everything needed to be in compliance with the laws. There are procedures I don't have a clue about.

"When the attempted robbery happened, I decided that there was no way I could continue being there by myself and successfully run the bank. If the bank was to continue, I needed help. That's when I wrote my advertisement and sent it off."

"So you advertised for a banker?" Mrs. Lasek was aghast.

"No, Mother, I'm not that foolish. I advertised for a bookkeeper. I never mentioned the bank, just that it was a successful business. I had several responses that I considered. Joel worked at a bank where he's from so he knows much more than I do about the workings. Not only that, but his priorities fit my needs for a husband."

"Why didn't you tell me you were contemplating this?" Joel didn't like the imperious tone Mrs. Lasek was using.

"Would you have approved of my plan this time, Mother?"

"Of course not."

"That's why I didn't. It's also why Joel and I were married today at the parsonage. I never thought I'd be married without any of my family with me, but your disapproval made it necessary." Tilde swiped at her face letting Joel know tears were slipping down her face.

"Mrs. Lasek, I know this is a shock," Joel began.

"A shock is putting it mildly, Mr. Richards. I'm flabbergasted, distressed, upset, disappointed to name only a few of the feelings and thoughts running through my mind at the moment. That my daughter would marry a stranger rather than discuss her difficulties with me. I simply don't know what to say."

"Mother, I did discuss it with you in May. You disapproved of the idea and didn't want to hear another thing about it. You also told me that in no way would you help me by working in the bank. I made the choice to do what needed to be done, with or without your support.

"Now, you have a choice to make. You can hold onto your disapproval or you can embrace my new life and my husband." Tilde rose so Joel stood too. "We are going upstairs to pack a bag for me. We will be staying in the inn tonight and maybe a few more days."

She led the way out of the room leaving Mrs. Lasek sitting alone in the parlor.

Tilde stood looking out her bedroom window, her hands covering the sides of her face. Silverpines lay before her. The house was up the slope that started near the river and rose to the mountains. There was evidence of repairs to some homes and businesses. Others had been abandoned. That was a headache she'd worry about another day.

Hands slipped up her arms to rest on her shoulders.

"Are you all right?"

"I knew it would be hard and that she wouldn't approve, but her vitriol was difficult to take."

Joel turned her to face him. She wiped the tears from her cheeks. Without any protest from her, he pulled Tilde against him and hugged her. His tender care burst the dam holding back her sobs. As she cried, Joel rubbed her back and murmured softly in her ear.

When she was all cried out, Joel released her but held her hand. He led her to the settee in the turret. The windows were open and a breeze cooled the room.

"I lost my father and brother in the earthquake and now I'm losing my mother." She pulled her handkerchief from her sleeve. Why she hadn't before Tilde had no idea. It was one of those ladylike things her mother was always coaching her about.

"She's upset for several reasons right now. I'm sure she'll accept this sooner or later. We will just have to be patient. This is a shock to her. Remember, she lost her husband and son."

"Yes, I know." Tilde blew her nose. "I just wish she was more supportive. I know she loves me and I love her. That's why it's so hard."

A knock sounded on the door which immediately opened. Dara Conway, the housekeeper, cook, and former nanny for Tilde and her brother came swiftly into the room.

"Auch, I be hearin' that ya done gone and gotten yourself married t'day. Your mother's that upset, she is. I'm a thinkin' it be a good thing for ya, I am." She rushed over to the settee and pulled Tilde up into a tight hug. "I know herself is upset but that'll pass. You just start your new life and be happy."

As Tilde was held tightly in Dara's arms, she said, "Thank you. I truly appreciate your support. You know Mother. She is a force to be reckoned with."

"That she is. That she is." Dara released Tilde and turned to look at Joel. "So t'is himself, is it? You certainly picked a handsome one." She squinted one eye at him. "I'm Dara Conway. I helped raise the lass you wed today. You'll be takin' good care of her or you'll be answerin' to me."

Joel stood. "Joel Richards, ma'am, at your service. I most certainly will do my best to be a good husband to Tilde." He winked at Dara. "And if I have any difficulties I'll be coming to you for advice."

"Hey, now." Tilde fisted her hands on her hips and grinned. "It's not fair for you to gang up on me with Dara. Who will I go to if I have difficulties with you?"

"Auch, Sweeting, you can always be a countin' on me when you're in need." Dara kissed Tilde's cheek. "Now, we'd best be packin' what you want to be takin' with you. Whether you want my advice or not, I'm goin' to be givin' it to you.

"Just pack enough for tonight and tomorrow. Then you both can come after work to get what you need for the next day. That'll give you and herself the chance to speak and I'll make sure she asks you to stay for supper. We can do that for a few days and I'll be tryin' my best to get her to ask you to start your living together here at the House.

"I be a thinkin' that herself is fearful of losin' her only child. That be why she t'were so against you writin' that advertisement. She's fearful of bein' alone."

Tilde looked at Joel. He lifted an eyebrow. She remembered his similar words before Dara arrived. "What do you think, Joel?"

"I think it's mighty fine advice and suggest we take it. I know you don't want to be estranged from your mother and I don't want that either. We can use these next few days to ease her into accepting our marriage."

Tilde kissed Dara on the cheek. "Will you help me decide what to take and help me pack?"

"Of course, Sweeting." Dara shot Joel a cocky smile. "You just be a sittin' there lookin' out at the town. We'll be gatherin' the things for your wedding night."

Heat rose up Tilde's neck and spread across her face. She knew she was blushing for about the millionth time today. And it wasn't over yet.

CHAPTER FIVE

FOLLOWING TILDE UP THE STAIRCASE in the inn, Joel watched the gentle sway of her hips. Her skirts hugged her shape and he swallowed down the desires that filled him. She was definitely all woman. He'd never thought his wedding night would continue his celibacy. Not only did he know she was nervous, but they'd only just met. He was now married to a stranger. Tonight was going to lead to blushes by both of them, most likely.

When they left Lasek house, Tilde's mother looked at them from the window of the parlor. She looked so forlorn Joel nearly told Tilde to go back inside. She must have had an inkling as to his thoughts, or maybe even fought within herself to do the same, as she grabbed his hand, hurrying them down the steps.

They had eaten supper at the inn dining room. When Mrs. Karson, whom Tilde called Ella Grace, found out they had been married that day she brought out two large pieces of angel food cake covered in blueberry compote and whipped cream.

"Everyone should have cake on their wedding day," Ella Grace had said. Then she leaned close to Tilde's ear and whispered, "How's your mother taking this?" Joel could hear since her whisper wasn't very soft.

"Not very well. Please pray she comes to accept this." Tilde accepted the squeeze of her friend's hand.

"I most certainly will."

Tilde stopped at the top of the stairs. "Um, ah, which room is ours?"

"Here." Joel unlocked the door. Should he pick her up and carry her across the threshold? He decided that was more intimate than he wanted, knowing it would make her even more nervous. Pushing the door wide, Joel bowed slightly, sweeping his arm indicating she should proceed him in. The bellboy had brought her bag up and it set in the middle of the floor.

"Um, ah, where's the bed?"

Joel watched the color stain Tilde's face. He wished he'd started counting how many times she'd blushed that day. He decided to start now since he was sure this wouldn't be the last one.

"This is a two-room suite. I think it's called the Governor's Suite. I thought we might like the extra space and, um, privacy."

Tilde looked at him quizzically. "Privacy?"

"To change. We can each have a room to change in." Joel felt his own cheeks heat. Now he was blushing. Being alone with a woman he'd met only hours ago seemed to be affecting him also. It struck him as funny. He grinned, then chuckled.

"What's so funny?"

"You've been blushing all day. I don't know how many times. Now I'm doing it too. I've never been alone in a hotel room with a woman before. Let alone one I only met today." He grabbed her bag and smiled at her.

Tilde smiled back. Then she laughed. "I know what you mean. I think it's something that has happened in town a lot in the past few months. There have been a lot of couples marrying without knowing each other much, if at all. That could lead to lots of blushing, at least for a while."

"I'm sure you're right. Let me show you the bedroom. You can change in there and I'll change in here."

This time it wasn't pink staining her cheeks, instead she blanched. "Um, ah, okay. That sounds good. Is it time to… yet?" He didn't know if that counted as a blush or not.

Joel lifted an eyebrow. "Can't say go to bed?"

"Um, no. I don't think I can." She looked him straight in the eye. Then she started giggling. "This is not how I ever pictured my wedding day. Married to a stranger, my mother furious with me."

Joel watched the humor slip from her expression.

"My father not there to walk me down the aisle." Her eyes filled with tears.

Dropping her bag, Joel took her in his arms. "Let it out, honey. According to my sister, every girl dreams of her wedding day. Yours hasn't lived up to your dreams, has it."

Tilde held on to him, crying. When she quieted, she looked up. "Thank you. You seem to understand so well."

Joel brushed the tears on her cheeks away with gentle fingers. "I don't have many memories of my birth mother, but the sadness is burned into my soul. Maybe it's made me more aware of it in others." He released her when she pulled back. "Or maybe it's my sister, Annie, telling me not to be an insensitive lout and remember all the reasons why you wanted a husband. She warned me with threats of pain and death if I made this day more difficult for you."

Tilde giggled. "Sounds like a girl I'd like to know."

"She's something, I'll say that. Maybe we'll be able to go to Cottonwood sometime. I'd like you to meet my family."

"I think I'd like that."

~~~~~

Rather than change and get into the bed, since it was early and still light out, they went for a walk through town. Tilde told him details of the earthquakes and their aftermath. There was quite a lot of repair work being done, but there were also empty houses and businesses. Tilde explained that many families had left since work was scarce as the town rebuilt. The bank held the mortgages for most of them.

With the setting of the sun, they went back to the inn. Joel now stood in the sitting room waiting for Tilde to let him know she was ready for bed. He had folded his clothes and set them on a table. How long did it take for a woman to change into a nightgown?

Walking to the door, Joel leaned his ear against it. He heard muttering that carried a tinge of frustrated annoyance. Not able to decipher the words he knocked on the door.

"Tilde, are you ready for me to come in?"

"No, yes. Oh bother. Come in. I need some help."

He stepped back as the door was pulled open. Tilde was standing in her unmentionables. He knew she was well covered in her drawers, chemise, and corset, as well as her stockings and shoes. It seemed all she'd removed were her bodice, skirt, and petticoats.

"I don't know how many times I've told Dara not to double knot the corset strings but she always does. At least I don't pull the laces tight. If I did, it could be dangerous if I fainted. I like to be able to breath."

She turned around and stomped over to the bed. "Will you please untie this cursed knot? Dara always helps me. I wonder if she double knots hers. She doesn't have anyone to help her. Well, from now on I'll be tying and untying my own laces. I don't know why she knots them anyway. It's not as if they are going to come untied with my petticoats and skirts covering the laces. Not to mention the corset cover." She stood with her back to him and gave a little wave toward the laces.

Joel stood staring at the bright pink corset. He'd always thought they would be white or black. This one was pink and gold brocade with thick gold stitches marching around the top and bottom. He wondered if they had a purpose or were just for decoration. Also if they were on the front. Her laces were gold too. Who would have thought that something only the wearer and maybe mother, sibling, or maid would see was so pretty? Well, he'd heard the soiled doves wore brightly colored corsets, but a modest young lady? His wife?

Tilde turned slightly and shot an annoyed eye at him. "Close your mouth, you look like a cod fish. Now, untie this cursed knot."

Joel hadn't realized his jaw had dropped. He closed his mouth and cleared his throat. "Yes, ma'am." Stepping behind her, he picked the double knot out and pulled the loop, untying the bow.

Joel watched as her hands quickly loosened the laces, then she moved them to the front and the corset came off and was hung over the foot rail of the bed. Tilde stretched her arms up and leaned from side to side. Even with the chemise covering her from shoulder to knee, Joel had to swallow down the desire that flared.

Tilde turned around. "Oh, um, thank you." Red flamed her cheeks. Joel fought the grin at another of her blushes. *That's two or three if I count her paling when we first spoke of going to bed.*

"Um, can you leave now and let me finish changing? Please?"

"Oh, yes, of course." Joel backed up, keeping his eyes on her. It was only a few steps, but he bumped into the wall beside the door. He could tell Tilde was fighting a grin. He moved sideways and pulled the door closed, shutting her from his view.

~~~~~

Sleep slowly released Tilde from its hold. She lay on her side listening to the birds greet the day outside the open windows. Then she realized something wasn't right. Her eyes popped wide open.

SHE WASN'T ALONE IN HER BED!!! An arm was around her waist holding her to the person behind her.

Stiffening with a jerk, Tilde's head cracked into the chin of whoever was behind her.

"Ouch!"

Tilde recognized Joel's pained cry and the events of yesterday came into focus in her mind. She turned, moving away from his hold. "Oh, I'm so sorry. Did you bite your tongue? Do you need a cold wet cloth to hold against it?"

She knew she was babbling, just as she had last night when Joel had to help her with the corset knot. That was so embarrassing, not even being able to untie her own corset. He must think she was a bungling idiot. First the knot, and now smacking him in the chin with her head. His arm slipped from her waist. The warmth of it fading as the morning air cooled the fabric of her nightgown.

Joel's expressive eyebrow lifted giving her a moment of unease, then she saw the twinkle in his eye. "No, but I bit my lip."

He's not going to want me to kiss it better, is he? The thought both scared and enticed her. Drat, she felt heat begin its climb up her neck. She scooted away from him, stopping only when she felt the edge of the bed nearing. The last thing she wanted was to fall to the floor.

"That's one. Be careful. You falling out of bed would hurt more than when I bumped into the wall." The twinkle was even more evident in his eyes.

Tilde nodded and slipped out of bed. She grabbed the wrapper she'd laid out on a nearby chair last night, putting it on. When she turned around, Joel was leaning back against the headboard with his arms behind his head. His nightshirt was unbuttoned at the neck leaving a few inches of his chest exposed to her gaze. The heat from her cheeks had been fading but now it flamed again.

"That's two," Joel said with a wide smile.

"Two what?"

"Blushes. I didn't think to count them until last evening. Today, I'm starting right now. You've already blushed twice and we've only been awake two minutes. Doesn't bode well for your cheeks for the rest of the day."

She wanted to respond to his teasing with a witty reply but felt another blush coming. Instead, she turned her back to him to hide it and walked to the washstand. "I'm going to wash up and begin dressing. You can leave now."

A chuckle right behind her as she picked up the pitcher made her hand shake, knocking it against the basin. Joel's hand came around and covered hers on the handle. "That seems a little heavy. Let me help you." As they poured the water, Tilde felt Joel's breath by her ear. "That's three," he whispered.

He was right. She was blushing again. When they set the pitcher down and his hand released hers, Tilde swung around and smacked him on the chest. "You get out of here. I'm... um, hungry, so get your clothes on."

Joel laughed, heading to the door. He gave her a quick smile, opened the door, and just as he closed it said, "That's four."

Tilde covered her cheeks with her hands. He was right.

CHAPTER SIX

THEY SPENT THE MORNING GOING over accounts at the bank. Tilde explained the number of accounts and mortgages that were abandoned or hadn't had a payment made since the disaster. Joel jotted facts and thoughts down in a notebook. They were interrupted a number of times when Tilde's friends came into the bank excited about her marriage.

"Tilde Lasek, how dare you not tell me so I could be at your wedding." Sarah Dekum stood with her hands on her hips when Tilde came from the office where they'd been working.

"Hey, you ran away and got married, not telling anyone. At least I stayed in town."

Sarah laughed. "You got me there."

Tilde had gone out from behind the counter and the girls hugged. She looked back and saw Joel standing in the office doorway. "Joel, come and meet one of my good friends. She owns the gun shop."

"Well, my husband and I do. He's holding down the fort while I come and see if you are good enough for my friend."

Joel came out and extended a hand to Sarah. "Pleased to meet you. I haven't met many of Tilde's friends."

They chatted for a few minutes. "I need to be going. Mason is working on a new gun, so I need to mind the store." She pulled a small revolver from her pocket. "You be good to Tilde or I just might use this sweet thing on you."

Joel held up his hands even though she was not pointing it at him. "Don't worry, I'll be good to her. No need for that, although I'd like to see it."

Sarah handed the small revolver to him.

"Smith and Wesson. What's the caliber?"

".38. It's a 38 Special"

"Very nice gun." He handed it back.

"My husband makes them. He was married to Mr. Wesson's daughter before she died. He's now the exclusive manufacturer and distributor for Smith and Wesson in the West. We're building a factory outside of town. We're hoping it brings more families to Silverpines.

"I'm sure it will. I'll be around soon to meet your husband."

"I'm sure he'll appreciate that." Sarah looked at Tilde. "He likes my gun. He'll do."

Tilde scoffed then hugged her friend. "Get out of here. We have work to do."

"Yes, ma'am." The girls giggled as Sarah left.

"She seems nice," Joel said as they walked back to the office.

"She is. We grew up together. There are several of the girls my age who might show up this morning. Tonya Watts, she owns the lumber mill and yard, and also owns the logging forest. She's married to Braylon Watts. He's converting the mill so it can generate electricity.

"You know Abby James. Betsy is Sheriff Sewell's wife. She won't be coming in. She's having a difficult confinement and is on bed rest. That's something I need to do. Go visit her. Maude Jones will scold me if I don't. She's another good friend. She helps with Betsy in the morning with Tonya and teaches the little girls at Howard House. It's an orphanage for girls. She grew up there."

As they settle into their chairs, the bank door opened again. "Tilde, where are you? I want to meet your new husband. Abby came by this morning while I was visiting Betsy. Tonya and Maude were there. Betsy says to get yourself over to her house, both of you. She wants to meet him too." Katie Deidmann came through the gate and into the office before Tilde and Joel could even rise. Katie threw her arms around Tilde. "I didn't even know you had sent an advertisement and here you are married. What a shock! How did your mother take it? Don't tell me. I know. She hates the idea."

"I was just saying the same thing."

"That your mother hates that you married?"

"No, silly. That I needed to go see Betsy." She looked at Joel. "Maybe we could go once the bank is closed."

He nodded, not able to get a word in since Katie started talking again.

"I need to leave. The twins are probably driving Miss Edie crazy. See you later. It was a pleasure meeting you, Tilde's husband. I still can't believe you got married and your mother didn't know." Katie hurried out of the office.

Tilde and Joel looked at each other and laughed.

"Is she always like that?"

"No, not always but when she gets excited, well, you saw."

Just before noon, Dara came in carrying a basket. Joel rushed forward to relieve her of the burden. "I brought you some lunch. I figured you'd be busy today, what with himself learnin' about the bank and everyone wantin' to see the new citizen of Silverpines." Dara went through the gate to behind the counter and gave Tilde a hug.

Joel raised his eyebrow. Tilde knew he was wondering about Katie's and Dara's boldness at not staying in the customer area. She just hugged the woman and smiled at him.

"Let's go into the office. We can eat at the desk. Will you be eating with us, Dara?" Tilde cleared the desk, gathering the papers and folders and tapping them into a neat pile.

"No, Sweeting, I'll be a goin' back to tend to herself. She's mighty pensive, that she is. Didn't hardly eat a thing last night or this morn. Stood lookin' out the window of the parlor last evening." Dara began setting containers and plates onto the desk. Joel poured lemonade from a jar into glasses.

Tilde looked at Joel. Tears clogged her throat. She loved her mother, even though she drove Tilde crazy with her scolding to be more ladylike. He set the jar down and took her hand, giving it a comforting squeeze.

"I'm a thinkin' you both might want to be a comin' at supper time this evening. You'll be needin' to get some clothing for tomorrow, and just maybe I can convince herself to be invitin' you to stay and eat. She can be savin' face, and you, Mr. Richards, can be gettin' to know herself a bit. Who knows where that could lead."

Tilde turned hopeful eyes at Joel.

"I think that's a very good idea, Mrs. Conway."

"Auch, be a callin' me Dara. We're family now. Well, I'll be leavin' you to your meal. Please, bring it all back home with you, will you, Sweeting?"

"We will. Thank you, Dara. This was quite thoughtful of you." Tilde gave the housekeeper a hug.

"T'wasn't anything I wouldn't do for my girl. You be a knowin' that." Dara patted Tilde on the cheek and left.

"Do you think Mother will welcome us and invite us to supper?"

"I don't see how she can't. I don't think Dara will allow anything else." Joel grinned, making Tilde chuckle.

"I think you're right. She is a force to be reckoned with. She can manipulate my mother into doing just what she wants, and Mother never knows it wasn't her idea." Tilde drew her eyebrows together. "I think she does that with me too, now that I think about it."

Joel just laughed, making Tilde slap him softly on the arm.

~~~~~

Mrs. Lasek sat at the head with Tilde on her left and Joel on her right, sitting in the middle of the long table. The stiffness of her smile wasn't very welcoming. She'd already been seated at the table when they arrived promptly at five fifty-five.

Tilde had stalled as long as Joel allowed. She had told him that supper was served at the specified time and being late was not an option. Still she'd dallied with her hair, pretended to misplace her gloves, and decided she needed a new handkerchief just as they were leaving the hotel room. Joel was sympathetic but didn't want to alienate his new mother-in-law, any more than he already had, by being late.

Not bothering to knock, Tilde had gone right into the house. Dara came bustling in welcoming them and saying herself was in the dining room. Joel was carrying her bag and set it on the floor by the stairs before going into the dining room. Now they sat in silence as Dara brought fragrant dishes in and placed them on the table.

"This be one of my Sweeting's favorite meals. Pork chops, applesauce, scalloped potatoes, peas, and Mother Lee's rolls. There be fresh peach pie for dessert." Dara set the basket of rolls in front of Joel. "Mind you have to be eating a good supper to have dessert." She patted him on the shoulder as she headed back to the kitchen.

Grace was said by Mrs. Lasek and the dishes were passed with murmured thank-yous until all plates were filled. The tension emanating from Mrs. Lasek could be cut with a knife. Her shoulders were ramrod straight. Her movements stiff as she cut her meat and began eating. They continued eating in silence.

Joel cleared his throat. "Thank you for inviting us for supper, Mrs. Lasek. We appreciate your hospitality."

"This is Tilde's home. She is always welcome here."

"Mother, does that mean my husband is not welcome?" Tilde set her fork down on her plate and looked at Joel.

Mabel set her silverware down and pulled a handkerchief from her sleeve. She touched it to her eyes. "Yes, he is welcome as you are, my dear. It's just..." She stopped speaking and looked from her daughter to Joel and back. "I'm having a difficult time adjusting to..." She stopped again, bringing the handkerchief up and pressing it to her lips. It was obvious she was struggling to keep back her tears. She reached a hand across and grasped Tilde's. "I've lost so much. I never thought I'd not attend my only daughter's wedding."

Joel watched as Tilde's eyes filled.

"I never wanted that either, Mother. I wanted you there so badly, but I knew you wouldn't approve of my actions and I couldn't deal with your objections. I was nervous enough marrying a stranger. Papa wasn't there.

Neither was Terrance. No one I love was there. Well, Mrs. Edmondson was there, but she's not family. I so wanted your support but it wasn't there, so I had to do what I knew was best without you."

"I'm so sorry. I lost Dexter and Terrance. I can't bear the thought of losing you too."

Joel wanted to say that her disapproval of Tilde's plans and needs were driving her daughter away. Instead he kept his mouth full of the delicious rolls.

"You aren't losing me, Mother. I love you and want to stay close like we were before. But now I have a husband and he needs to be included in your life if you want me in yours."

Mabel released Tilde's hand, pulling hers back and dropping it into her lap, hiding it from view. Joel thought she might be clenching them together. She definitely didn't look pleased with Tilde's words.

The green eyes, so large in his wife's face, looked at him, pleading for him to say something. He didn't know what would help the situation. He sent up a quick prayer for the right words.

"Mrs. Lasek, I'm not trying to take your daughter away from you. I came to Silverpines to marry her in order to help her as a bookkeeper. I think the Lord brought me here to facilitate Tilde in keeping the bank profitable and able to support you both. The tragedy that took so many men, including your husband and son, needn't cause you to lose your business, too.

"That aside, I promise to be a good, God-fearing

husband to your daughter. I want to be an asset to you, also. I know there is no way I can replace those you've lost. I hope I can be a comfort to you and give you security knowing that Tilde is treated well. She deserves no less than a faithful, committed husband, and I will do my best to be that man for her."

Mabel looked between them again. She swallowed, then took a deep breath. "Are you going to find a house to live in? Are you going to leave me here in this huge house all alone?"

Joel looked at Tilde.

"We haven't discussed it, Mother. We can't stay at the inn forever. We will have to decide on some place rather soon."

"Would you... I know I haven't been very welcoming or supportive." She looked at Joel. "I'll understand if you don't want to consider it, but if you would like to live here, I will do all I can to make you welcome. I do believe the house is large enough for all of us."

Joel shot a glance at Tilde. There was doubt and hope on her face. "We will give your offer serious consideration. It is something we need to discuss between the two of us."

That they hadn't immediately jumped at the offer showed as disappointment in Mabel's face and the slight slump of her shoulders.

"We'll talk and pray about it tonight and no doubt tomorrow, Mother. Shall we come for supper tomorrow?"

"Yes, of course, please do." Rather than the derision and disappointment in her tone there was resignation tempered with a small dose of hope.

"I can't promise we will have made a decision by then," Tilde said.

That tiny bit of hope dimmed in Mabel's eyes. Tilde's caution was merited, Joel thought. It would be a total turn around for Mrs. Lasek to be welcoming to him living in her house with her daughter. He figured it would take quite a bit of prayer by everyone, including Dara, to know what the best thing was for him and Tilde to do.

CHAPTER SEVEN

IT TOOK TILDE AND JOEL four more days before they agreed to move into Lasek House. They decided the day after that first supper to move in but chose not to let Mabel know for a few days. The extra days were to give them time to get to know each other better without outside influences, be they Tilde's mother or Dara. Once they moved their privacy would be limited to their bedroom.

Each evening they went for supper. The tension was less but not gone all together. Both Tilde and Joel appreciated the effort Mabel was making to be welcoming and get to know him. That her questions sometimes sounded more like an inquisition than polite conversation he pushed aside, answering openly.

Joel could tell that Mabel dearly loved Tilde. He was beginning to see that she was similar in personality to Mrs. Taylor back in Cottonwood. He was experienced with strong-minded, intense women. It didn't take much to please them, even though many would disagree. They were insecure and needed to be listened to and their thoughts and feelings acknowledged. By doing so, they were happy or at least satisfied they'd been heard. He was going to do that as much as his ability and patience allowed.

Hearing the bank door open, Joel looked out the office door. He'd moved the desk so he could see most of the bank when he was sitting at it. Tilde had insisted he take over as president. He'd been reluctant to do so but as he'd watched over the few days he'd been there, it was clear many of the men and some of the women who came didn't consider Tilde's thoughts and comments to be taken seriously. He had to admit she was timid when doing more than telling, even though her instincts and knowledge were sound.

Seeing that it was Sarah Dekum, owner of the gun shop, he focused back on the ledger before him. Sarah had lost her father in the disaster and married Mason Dekum back in early June. She was no threat to his wife.

That Tilde was his wife was cemented into his being, even though they had only been married a few days. It wasn't love yet, but he thought that could come. Sleeping next to her each night was more than pleasant. He hoped that they could progress to more intimacy soon.

Then again, maybe he should press it a little since tomorrow they were moving to Lasek House. It would be Saturday and the bank closed at noon. They would be able to settle into whatever room Mrs. Lasek decided.

Tilde hoped she would give them the master bedroom, but Joel thought that was unlikely. It would take more time for her to give up the room she'd spent so many years in. It would also relinquish her role as mistress of the house.

He glanced up, looking at Tilde as she completed her transaction and said goodbye to Mrs. Dekum. The profile of his wife made him swallow. She was so beautiful. Hair a dark auburn that was swept up in loops and swirls, he had no idea how she kept it in place. He knew it framed her heart-shaped face, set off by a long graceful neck. His fingers fidgeted to stroke her cheek, the color of her skin reminding him of a pale pink rose in his mother's garden. Even her blushes were simply a darker variation.

Then there were her eyes, deep forest green reminding him of the pine forests he rode through on the train. Large and wide open, they were rimmed with lashes the color of her hair as were her arched eyebrows. Her smiles lit them up and her laughter caused them to sparkle. Joel had noticed that Tilde had her mother's eyes, though her hair color must have come from her father. Mabel's hair was light brown.

Joel let his gaze slip to her figure. He swallowed again. She was definitely a woman. Curves in all the right places. He knew her shape wasn't due to tight lacing of her corset. None of her curves were padded either.

And she was soft. Though they went to sleep on their separate sides of the bed, by morning her back was snuggled against his chest, his arm around her waist. The first two mornings she jumped away from him when she woke. Now, she'd wiggle just a little bit closer before she let him know she was awake. He was always awake a little earlier and enjoyed simply holding her.

Yes, he would see if she was ready to move into the more physical aspects of their marriage.

~~~~~

Tilde went back to her desk as Sarah closed the door behind her. She glanced up as she sat and saw Joel looking at her. There was a look on his face that brought a blush to hers. He was so attractive both in form and personality. At the moment it was his form she was drawn to.

Slightly above average height, he was lean but muscular. He'd told her he did calisthenics several times a week. He planned on getting dumbbells as he'd left his behind for his brothers to use.

Dark brown hair parted slightly off center matched his facial hair. Tilde wondered if the mustache and beard would tickle if she kissed him. The thought made her blush which caused Joel's eyebrow to rise. Drat her blushes. That eyebrow was so very expressive.

With hair as dark as it was she would have thought he'd have brown eyes. Instead they were so light a gray they were silver. A circle of nearly black rimmed the iris. Tilde wondered if they would darken to stormy when he became angry.

With her face heating, she sat quickly and focused on

adding up the column of numbers before her. She'd already added it twice. The standard set by her father was do each calculation six times or until you got six sums the same. After not getting the same total at all, she quit with a frustrated growl. It was almost time to close the bank. She'd balance the drawer and attempt this stupid column of numbers tomorrow.

While she was counting the cash, Joel came up behind her, making her fingers fumble. Something funny was going on in her insides. She didn't quite know what it was but she had a feeling she knew.

They were getting along very well. Getting to know each other. Liking each other. At least she liked him and thought he liked her. How long did one have to wait when one was married to begin... well... that aspect of marriage?

Tomorrow they were moving into Lasek House. Her mother and Dara lived there. Tilde wasn't sure how much privacy they would have. Would her mother enter their room without knocking? At times in the past she had. That wouldn't be welcome by Joel, she was pretty sure. Tilde didn't think she'd like it much either. She wasn't a little girl anymore. She was a woman. A married woman. She wanted to be treated like one. In all ways, she realized, and heat rose up her neck.

"Are you finished?" Joel asked, close behind her shoulder.

"Yes, it balances." Tilde was glad her voice didn't tremble in response to his nearness.

"I'll put it in the safe and lock it. Get your mantle and hat. We'll head to the inn." Joel took the drawer, doing as he'd said.

Normally, they stayed later, but Tilde agreed that they didn't need to today. She wanted to think it was because they needed to pack, but she had taken her things back to the house each day. Joel kept his things neatly in the one trunk he'd opened. There really wasn't much to pack.

"I'm, um, glad we decided to have supper at the inn. A last night to ourselves before we move home." Tilde pinned her hat in place. Joel took the mantle from its hook on the hall tree and draped it around her shoulders. He left his hands on her shoulders a few moments longer than necessary. Tilde could feel another blush beginning.

"I am too. The last night of our honeymoon."

Tilde suppressed a quiver. She didn't want him to know how his touch and words affected her. She looked down, drawing her gloves on.

Joel's hands gripped her shoulders again, turning her to face him. Fingers touched her chin, tilting her head back so she could see his face. His eyes, those silver eyes, told her his thoughts mirrored hers. She wanted him to kiss her. Wanted him to want her.

Slowly, his head lowered, as did Tilde's eyelids. The bristles of his mustache and beard tickled just before his lips touched hers. At first, the kiss was soft, slow as if waiting for her to pull back. When she didn't, his lips firmed on hers. His arm slipped around her, drawing her against him. Even through her garments she could feel his chest was solid, strong.

Tilde knew he used an aftershave but hadn't been this close to truly smell it. Sandalwood and cinnamon encircled her, welcoming her into his embrace. She lifted her arms to his back, spreading her fingers to maximize her touch.

Joel eased back, again softening the kiss. Two, then three small kisses brushed her lips. She opened her eyes and saw in his exactly what she desired. That tonight be a true honeymoon.

~~~~~

Tilde and Joel laughed as they entered the inn lobby. Halfway between the bank and the inn the rain that had been held in the gray clouds all day broke loose, drenching them as they ran along the boardwalk.

"We should have brought the umbrella with us," Tilde said as she shook wetness from her mantle.

The small hat she wore gave little protection and her hair was dripping and sagging, locks slipping from the pins. Joel couldn't resist. He plucked one from her cheek, twirling it around his finger. "And miss seeing you with your hair drenched and falling around your face. Never." He grinned mischievously. She laughed as she batted his hand away.

Ella Grace Karson, wife of the inn's owner, came around the desk. "Oh my, you did get caught in it, didn't you? Would you like baths drawn?"

"No, thank you, Mrs. Karson. But some extra towels would be appreciated," Joel gave her a slight bow as he and Tilde crossed the lobby. Tilde gave her friend a smile and a wave.

"Of course. I'll bring them right up."

Tilde ran up the stairs holding her skirts high. Joel watched her hips sway and hurried after her. He hoped it wouldn't take long for the towels to be delivered.

Laughing as she bounced on her toes, Tilde waited as he dug in his pocket for the key. "You could have had that out so I could start getting out of these wet things sooner."

The memory of her standing in her corset made his fingers fumble so he dropped the key. If things went the way he hoped, there would be new memories of her out of those wet things.

Finally getting the door unlocked, Joel stood in front of it. At Tilde's puzzled look, he swept her up in his arms. "In honor of our last night here, I'm carrying you over the threshold." That wasn't his entire reason but he didn't want Tilde to get shy by saying more. Her smile and the arm looped around his neck encouraged him that the afternoon might end the way he hoped.

"Aren't you going to put me down?" Tilde asked as he strode through the sitting room.

"Not yet." Joel gave her a quick kiss. Not paying quite enough attention, he knocked her feet on the door frame as he entered the bedroom. "Oops, sorry."

Tilde laughed. "No harm done."

He set her on her feet and began unhooking the frog closings of her mantle. The maroon velvet was wet and the satin frogs slipped as he worked to release them.

"I can do it," Tilde said.

"You work on your hat." Joel succeeded in removing her mantle and waited for her to unpin her hat. "I'll hang these in the sitting room. You start on your hair." He handed her a towel. "Dry it as best you can. I don't want you taking ill because of it."

"Yes, sir." Tilde saluted as she handed him her hat.

A knock sounded on the door as Joel hung his coat beside Tilde's mantle and hat. Ella Grace stood there with a pile of white terrycloth towels when he opened it.

"This should be enough to dry you both off. If you need more don't hesitate to ask." She winked at him as she turned to leave.

"Thank you." Joel closed and locked the door. He hesitated a moment before he crossed to the bedroom. Until now he'd always changed in the sitting room. He wanted to do so in the bedroom. He wanted to help Tilde out of her wet things. Wanted to remove his own. Deciding she could kick him out if she wanted, he carried the towels and entered the bedroom.

Tilde was sitting in front of the dresser looking into the attached mirror. Some locks of her hair were hanging down while others were still pinned somewhat in place. He came up behind her and set the towels down.

Her eyes met his in the mirror. The pupils were dilated. He read excitement, longing, uncertainty, and some trepidation in them.

She pulled another pin, allowing the damp lock to join the others. Joel picked it up, never taking his eyes from hers. "Your hair is beautiful. Even wet, it's soft."

"Thank you."

"Let me help." Joel found a pin and pulled it. Another lock fell. She took the pin from his fingers and placed it in a bowl on the dresser. He pulled another. Their eyes stayed locked. Every movement was done instinctively.

When the last lock lay on her shoulders, Joel took a towel and wrapped her hair, squeezing the dampness from it. As he massaged the towel over her scalp, Tilde's eyes fluttered shut. A blush lit her cheeks.

Joel abandoned her hair and pulled her to him, his arms encircling her shoulders. "Tilde, this is our last night here." Her eyes opened and found his in the mirror again. She turned in his arms.

"Yes, please," she answered his unasked question.

Joel did his best to keep the deepness of his kiss from scaring her. When her arms came around him, her hands burying themselves in his hair, he released his pent-up desires and allowed his to match what he felt coming from her.

CHAPTER EIGHT

"HAVE YOU GOT THAT TOTALED yet?"

Tilde looked up at Joel and stuck out her tongue. "Here, you do it. I've been busy all morning, just like every Saturday. People get paid on Friday and come to the bank on Saturday." She shoved the ledger toward him as he stood beside her.

Joel leaned down and whispered in her ear. "You haven't been distracted by our last night at the inn, have you?" When she blushed and smacked his arm, he laughed.

"Just go away and let me add."

"We could purchase a couple of adding machines. It makes things much easier. You just punch the numbers, pull the lever, and it adds it up. There's a paper tape which records it all, so you have a record of what you put in."

"I don't know. We've always done it this way. It works."

The door opened and three men in plaid flannel shirts came in.

"Hello, Mr. Bunyan. Well, all three Mr. Bunyans." Tilde started to rise from her seat, but Joel laid a hand on her shoulder.

"You stay here and get that sum finished. I'll tend to the Mr. Bunyans." Joel went to the teller window. "I'm Joel Richards, new husband to Tilde here. I'll be working here at the bank. How may I help you?"

The men studied Joel for several long seconds. "You'll do, I guess," the one in front said. "I'm Paul, this is Peter and that's James. We work at the lumber mill. Got the saw working again. Got paid yesterday so we thought we'd get us some bank accounts to put the money in."

"I can help you with that. Rather than do it here, let's go into my office. You can all do the paperwork at the same time." Joel took three bank books from a drawer and smiled at Tilde as they passed her desk.

"I could help with that, if you want me to," she said, her pencil tapping on the blotter.

"I think I can handle it, my dear. You can finish that sum." Joel's wink had Tilde pressing her lips together to keep from replying.

The opening of the three savings accounts was soon complete and Joel saw the men to the bank door. "Thank you," he said, shaking each man's hand. "Good luck with the sawmill. I'm glad it's running again."

"We are too. Glad we could all get jobs there. Our ma wanted us to stick together." Peter tipped his hat and jumped down the steps following his brothers into the street.

Joel closed the door and went behind the counter and leaned his hip on Tilde's desk. "You get that column to balance yet?" When she growled, he grinned. "Think about adding machines. We got them for Cottonwood Bank and it really helped with all the addition and subtraction."

Tilde just ignored him, tapping her pencil by each number in the column until she reached the bottom. She threw the pencil across the room. "That's it. I'm done for the day. I've fought this stupid ledger page for two days. I'm setting it aside until Monday."

Joel stroked his mustache to hide his grin. He'd leave the topic alone and let her come to her own conclusion as to the benefits of the adding machines.

"It's nearly noon anyway," he said. "Let's begin counting the cash and closing the safe. Your mother said she would hold dinner for us. I don't want to delay it and get on her bad side on the day we move in."

"Only you are moving in. I've lived there all my life." Tilde got up and went to pull the cash drawer from her teller window.

"That's true. I still don't want to be late." Joel went to his office and brought back the cash the Bunyan brothers had deposited. He waited until Tilde was finished balancing her drawer then they put the cash in the safe and closed it. He now knew the combination, so he could open it if Tilde wasn't there.

He helped her with her mantle and slipped his coat on. The weather was cool for late September. He hoped that didn't mean the winter would be colder than normal. Although cold nights would be welcome if Tilde snuggled close to him in bed.

~~~~~

Mabel Lasek was standing on the front porch as they walked up the steps. Though she was smiling, Tilde saw that it didn't reach her eyes. Her heart sank. It was evident her mother still wasn't happy about her marriage. All she could hope was that as she got to know Joel he would work his way into her heart. He certainly had to her own.

It wasn't love. It was too soon for that. Tilde had talked to Millie Cutler about marrying a stranger. Millie had done so to save the mercantile she owned. Also to have a father to her four children. What she got was the husband and five more children. That had been a shock when they stepped off the train.

Millie's advice was to do everything she could to make the marriage work. To support her new husband and get to know him, not presupposing she knew what he was thinking. So far that had been easy. Joel was a laid-back man, seeming to be content in his circumstances. Well, he was pushing for those adding machines. She'd think about it but wasn't convinced the new technology would be better than adding the numbers herself. But after the last two days, her frustration was mounting with her math skills.

"Hello, Mother. Thank you for meeting us."

"I wanted to welcome you back and your husband to his new home. Your trunks and bags were brought this morning. They are in your room, Tilde." Mabel turned to Joel. "Since we will be living together, I believe it would be appropriate to dispense with formal address. I will call you Joel, and you may call me Mother."

"Mother, he may not want to call you that. He has a mother."

"It's fine, Tilde. I call mine Mama. Sometimes Katie Mama. I'm pleased to call you Mother, Mrs. Lasek."

Joel slipped an arm around Tilde's waist. She leaned slightly into his side, not so much that her mother would notice. That would be most improper, for sure.

"Come," Mabel said. "Let's not keep Dara waiting. She's made pumpkin soup and apple pie." Mabel preceded them into the house and through to the dining room. She stepped aside and waved Tilde and Joel before her. "I relinquish my spot at the head of the table to you, Joel. Tilde, you may sit at the foot."

"Thank you, Mother," Joel said. "I accept the honor of the head of the table. However, when we are just family at the table, I would prefer you both sit on either side of me. I like that we would be closer, making conversation easier."

Tilde was surprised and grateful that her mother acknowledged her husband as the head of the house. Abdicating her place as the mistress had to be difficult.

She remembered the first time they ate in the dining room after the disaster. Her mother had sat down in her father's chair and they'd both wept at the change. Each evening since, Tilde sat in the middle on her mother's left looking across the table to the vacant place her brother used to occupy.

Tilde glanced sideways at her mother, wanting to see her reaction to Joel's suggestion of a closer arrangement of the place settings. Again, she was surprised. The softening of her face and the slight smile, that did reach her eyes, told Tilde her mother hadn't been eager to sit in Tilde's regular place.

"I think that is a wonderful suggestion." Tilde squeezed his hand. "With just us we can surely be less formal."

"I agree," Mother said. "If we have guests we will need to sit in our proper places, however."

"Of course." Joel held the chair for Mother and then went around to seat Tilde. When he was seated they sat in silence for a few moments. Mother cleared her throat and pointed to the crystal bell beside his place. "Oh, yes. Of course." Tilde could see a slight blush stain his neck as he lifted the bell and set it jingling.

It occurred to her that this would be the first time he was master of a house and head of the table. She glanced at her mother to see her reaction. An indulgent smile was on her lips. It gave Tilde hope that her mother would accept Joel as her husband and part of the family.

~~~~~

Wanted: Bookkeeper

Joel was standing in the bedroom, Tilde's bedroom, his open trunk sat beside the wall behind the door. He knew it was a good spot for it while he unpacked. The real issue was there was no place to put his clothing, let alone his other things. Tilde's dresser was filled with her things as were the drawers in the wash stand.

He'd been able to squeeze his suits into the wardrobe beside Tilde's garments. Now he needed to unpack his other clothing items. He had no place for his shirts and socks, let alone his underwear.

Frustration came out in a sigh and pursed lips. He placed his hands on his hips. Where was Tilde, anyway? Shouldn't she be helping him? Maybe clearing a few drawers from her dresser so he had somewhere to put his things? He was sure there were items in both the dresser and wardrobe she never wore. His sisters certainly had plenty.

Rather than stand here, alone, wondering where his wife was and getting nothing done, he left the room. The second floor had several bedrooms. Tilde had pointed out her mother's room the first day when they packed a bag to take to the inn. There were at least two more bedrooms. Tilde's was across the front of the house.

The door to another room was open. He moved to it and looked in. Tilde sat next to her mother on the bed. His wife's arm was around her shoulders.

"It's just so difficult," Mother was saying. "I lose your father and brother. Now you are leaving me."

"I'm not, Mother. We are living here. I'm not going

anywhere."

"I know, I'm just afraid you will. I'll be left all alone in this house with only empty rooms and memories." Mother wiped her eyes with her handkerchief. "I know your husband needs this dresser. He could probably use some of Terrance's things. I haven't done anything with his or your father's. I simply haven't been able to deal with it. Not been able to sort through them or pack them away in trunks."

Joel saw Tilde pat her mother on the back. "I know it's hard. I miss them so terribly too. I'll help you, if you want. With Joel here I should be able to take some time off like I did before."

Mother turned to her. Joel stepped back out of sight range. "You would do that?"

"Of course, I love you and we are both grieving. It would be a way we can help each other heal. I'll speak to him about taking Monday morning off." She nudged her mother's shoulder. "That way he can add up that stupid column I've been fighting for two days."

Joel stifled his laugh and stepped back into the doorway. "Excuse me. Am I interrupting?"

Tilde held out her hand to him. "No, of course not. We are emptying this dresser for your things. Once it's empty, you can move it into our room."

"Me? All by myself?" He grinned at Tilde, placing his hand on his chest as if affronted.

She picked up on his teasing. "You're the big strong man of the house. You should be able to do it without help from little ole me."

Joel puffed out his chest. "That's right, ma'am. I'm sure it won't be too much for me to handle."

Mother gave a small chuckle. "I'm sure that's correct. It is on wheels, after all."

Joel did an exaggerated deflation of his chest. "You wound my pride, madam."

"Most men need their pride wounded at times. I'll be happy to do so for you." She was smiling now. A true smile. It made her look more like Tilde.

Joel needed to remember that her world had been torn asunder not that long ago. She was grieving and Tilde had been so busy at the bank she hadn't been able to stay with her mother. They both needed time to grieve. Tilde had broken open her grief the day he arrived. Mabel probably hadn't succumbed to hers yet. Joel would do what he could so Tilde could spend time with her mother so they could grieve and heal together.

CHAPTER NINE

"GOOD MORNING, MISS. I'D LIKE to speak to someone about opening an account."

Joel didn't recognize the man's voice but that wasn't too unusual. He hadn't been in Silverpines that long. This man must be new, however, since he wanted to open an account. Joel stepped out of his office. "I'll be able to help you with that, Mr…"

"Jeremiah Henderson," Tilde squealed. She ran around the counter and hugged the man. "When did you get back to Silverpines? How long has it been? Let me think. Fourteen years."

"Yesterday. I'm looking into reopening Pike's Silver Mine." Jeremiah winked at Tilde, making Joel grit his teeth. He squashed the feeling of jealousy. She was just meeting an old friend. Jeremiah's next words eased away all concern.

"I'm also going to be marrying Maude."

"So you've got that hundred dollars, do you? I'm so

happy for you. She mourned for so long after you moved." Tilde hugged him again. "Jeremiah, I'd like you to meet my husband, Joel Richards. Joel, this is a friend from my childhood, Jeremiah Henderson."

"Pleased to meet you, Mr. Henderson."

"Come around here and Joel can show you into his office." Tilde held the gate open allowing him to come through.

Once they were settled in the office, Joel drew the paperwork and bank book from a drawer. "Welcome to Silverpines, Mr. Henderson. These papers need to be filled out and signed. How much are you depositing?"

"Five hundred thousand dollars will be arriving on the next train by armed courier."

Joel was speechless. The entire bank wasn't worth that much, at least not since the disaster. Mortgages hadn't been paid upon and some had been turned back to the bank. Businesses were just beginning to get back into regular operation.

Mr. Henderson laughed. "Surprised me, too. I didn't know about it until yesterday when my boss told me I owned part of Pike Silver Mine Consortium as well as another mine in New Mexico.

"We arrived yesterday to see if the mine is viable to reopen. I'm a mining engineer and I hope Mrs. Sewell will hire me to oversee its opening." Jeremiah began filling out the forms.

"I see," Joel said. He opened the bank book and filled in the name. "What's your address, or do you even have one yet?"

"No, I don't. I need to find a house as I'll be marrying soon. Do you know who I should talk to about that?"

Joel smiled. "You came to the right place. The bank now owns several houses as the families either died in the earthquakes, or had a loved one die and they left town, turning the house back to the bank. I can show you several."

It didn't take long to set up the account, with Jeremiah depositing a much lesser amount than would be coming in a few days.

"Let's talk with my wife about which houses would be best for you and your fiancé."

~~~~~

The bank door opened causing Tilde and Joel to look up. They'd been going over some papers at her desk with Joel leaning over while she sat.

"I just heard there's a no 'count little boy running the bank here in town."

Tilde glanced up and saw a smile broaden on Joel's face. He straightened and hurried around the counter. The man he hugged was tall and muscular. He wore a Stetson that had seen better days and lightly worn work clothes.

"Nathan Ryder, someone I never figured would be in the town of Silverpines. What brings you here? Come on back and meet my wife. Are Grace, Cindy, and the twins with you?"

"No, I'm here dealing with the silver mine. I seem to

own some stock in it. You met Jeremiah Henderson this morning, he tells me."

"Yes, I did. He opened an account and bought a house. Seems he came from here and is marrying a friend of Tilde's. Nathan, this is my lovely wife, Tilde Richards. Tilde, this is an old friend, and I stress the old, Nathan Ryder, otherwise known as The Preacher."

Tilde gasped. She'd heard of The Preacher. He was a legend. A minister who not only carried a gun but wasn't afraid to use it. He was also a U.S. Marshal with a reputation of being the fastest gun anyone knew.

"Wel… Welcome to Silverpines, Mr. Ryder."

"Nathan, did you know Clay Cutler and his family are living here now?"

"Found out this morning. Seems Clay helped this little lady not get captured when the bank was nearly robbed."

"Sheriff Sewell told me about that. Sounds like Ryder is beginning to have Callings too."

The men went on discussing the connections between the newer citizens of Silverpines and Nathan Ryder. How could so many men from so many places being related to or knowing him end up marrying women in Silverpines, Tilde wondered? She counted. Sheriff Sewell came from Ryder Mountain in Kentucky. Jeremiah Henderson just came back to town after working for Nathan. Clay Cutler and his children were second cousins. And Joel knew him from who knows where? She certainly didn't. That's four grown men and five children. To top that off, Nathan owned part of the mine. No one could write this even in a dime novel.

"You'll have to come for supper some evening. Maybe we could get everyone together at Lasek House. Imagine the tales we all could tell. Especially about Nugget Nate and Penny."

Nathan laughed. "That would be a hoot. We'll have to do that, but not yet. There are things afoot that need to be resolved first."

"You have a Calling?" Joel asked, now serious.

"Yes, that's why I'm here. Soon as it's resolved we'll plan that hoedown, as Nate would say. Now, I'm wanting a short-term deposit made. Don't like leaving that amount of money in the railcar safe. I'm also wanting to take a look at the Pike Silver Mine Consortium books. We're thinking there may be some fraud going on."

"Certainly, come on into my office and I'll get you all set up."

Tilde opened and closed her mouth several times as she watched them head away. Would wonders never cease? Nathan Ryder, U.S. Marshal and The Preacher here in her bank.

~~~~~

"I'm going to get this stupid ledger balanced if it kills me," Tilde grumbled. "But first I'm putting more coal in the boiler. Who would have thought it would get so cold in October? I hope it's just a day or two." She stood, throwing her pencil onto the offending ledger.

It seemed that ever since Joel had come to Silverpines

her mathematic skills had regressed to first grade level. It seemed as if each ledger had a mind of its own and changed the numbers every time she tried to add the column.

To top it off, Joel had stopped mentioning the adding machines. Instead, he just raised his eyebrow whenever he heard her complaining. That eyebrow and the tiny grin made her want to throw the ledger at him. Every time. Her mother's strict teachings on propriety were all that kept her from injuring her husband.

Tilde stomped down the stairs into the basement. Last winter her father had installed a boiler and radiator system to heat the bank. Someone had to come down periodically during the day to add more coal. They banked the coals at night so they were still hot in the morning. Tilde didn't like shoveling the dirty black rocks into the firebox, but Joel was out of the bank at the moment, so the job fell to her. Or she could be cold waiting for him to return.

When she spilled coal dust on her skirt it was all she could do not to swear like a logger. She was able to finish stoking without any more temptations, but she grumbled again as she climbed back to the main floor. Just as she closed the basement door behind her, the bank door opened and Millie Cutler came in. Three little girls followed her in. One had a magnifying glass in front of her eye making it appear quite large.

"Good morning, Tilde. Whatever have you been doing? You're covered in black dust."

"Stoking the boiler downstairs. Joel is gone at the moment or he would have done it. I was too cold to wait." Tilde excused herself and went into the small retiring room and washed her hands. A quick look in the mirror showed that she did have coal dust on her white shirtwaist as well as her blue and white striped skirt. There was a smudge on her face which was removed with a quick swipe of a wet washcloth.

"Now, how may I help you?" Tilde said as she came to the teller window.

"Miss Tilde, can I look at your dust? I've never studied it before?" Grace Cutler asked, the magnifying glass pressed against her cheek.

"I want to look too, Grace," the littlest of the girls, Ida, said.

"May I, not can I," corrected Millie, "and no, you may not. I just did wash and I'm not eager to do it again."

Grace twisted her lips to the side in irritation. Ida looked disappointed too. Opal wasn't paying any attention. She was standing quietly, gripping a drawstring bag in her hands.

"So, what brings all you ladies to the bank today?" Tilde leaned over the counter to better see all the girls. The two older ones were five and Ida was three.

"I'm going to open a savings account," Opal said, holding up her bag. "I've saved five dollars. I think it will be safer from the boys if it's in the bank."

Tilde kept her expression neutral, not wanting to

chuckle at the disgust flooding Opal's face. It might hurt the girl to think she was being laughed at. "You are most certainly correct. My brother got into my piggy bank more times than I want to think about when I was your age."

Tilde and Millie exchanged compassionate eyes. Millie knew Tilde had lost her father and brother in the disaster. Millie had lost her husband. Clay Cutler came to Silverpines after answering Millie's ad in the Groom's Gazette.

"We can open your account and you will have a book where each time you deposit or withdraw any money we'll record it in your book and in the one we keep at the bank. That's how we'll know how much money you have." Tilde showed the girls the bank book she took from the drawer.

"Is Mr. Richards here?" Opal stretched on tiptoe trying to see over the tall counter. "I want him to help me."

"I'm sorry. He's out of the bank for a while. I can help you. Come around and we'll work at the desk. Are either of you opening an account too?" She held the gate open allowing Opal through.

"Not today. Grace spent her money on a new doll. Ida hasn't enough to deposit yet," Millie said. "I have a deposit, but I can wait until you have helped Opal."

"I really wanted Mr. Richards to help me. He's real handsome." Opal leaned close and whispered, "I know he's married to you but don't worry. He's too old for me anyway. I just wanted him to help me. You can though. I don't mind."

Tilde coughed to hide her giggle. "Thank you. Let's get this book filled out."

It didn't take long to set up the account and to handle Millie's deposit. Soon she watched as Millie herded the girls up the street, Opal's bank book clutched tightly in her hand.

Tilde went back to her desk and took up her pencil again. Maybe the stupid columns would add up and balance this time.

~~~~~

Joel walked slowly back to the bank. Now that he'd visited every house the bank held a mortgage on he had a better idea of how to proceed. The only house that was sold recently was the one Jeremiah Henderson purchased last month. It was late October and some of the houses had been abandoned since April. Others whose families still lived in them hadn't made a payment since the earthquakes that had killed so many. This couldn't continue or the bank might fail.

With the marriages and the mill working again, some were up to date or near it on their mortgages. There was work going on at the collapsed mine in hopes of reopening it. At the moment the focus was on recovering the bodies of those killed.

New people were coming to town or returning slowly, as jobs were becoming available. Braylon Watts, the man who married Antonia Woodson, the mill owner, was bringing electricity to the town. He was planning to somehow use the mill wheel to generate the electricity. Already poles were being erected and lines strung. Joel wondered if Mabel Lasek would allow him to have the house wired for lights and ceiling fans. He'd looked at some catalogues Clay Cutler had at the mercantile.

Joel planned to have the bank wired and an alarm system set up to ring if the bank was broken into at night. He wouldn't mention it to Tilde yet. She seemed reluctant to make any changes to the bank in its policies and methods.

Though she didn't like many of his ideas, Joel enjoyed, no loved being married to Tilde. Other than the differences in their ideas about the bank, they worked well together. They were getting along well within their marriage too. The more intimate aspects were wonderful. Joel made sure Tilde was satisfied and enjoyed their times together. He most certainly did.

Joel tipped his hat to Mrs. Edmondson as they passed on the boardwalk. There was talk of having the streets cobbled. If Silverpines did so they would put in sidewalks too, at least in the business district.

Progress was returning to Silverpines. He'd had inquiries about a few of the abandoned houses. That brought his thoughts back to the dilemma he had: what to do about the unpaid mortgages of the abandoned houses and the non-payments of those still occupied. He had some plans to consider and calculations to do before he presented his ideas to Tilde. He hoped she'd be willing to listen and try them out. He wasn't very optimistic since she still refused to consider the adding machines.

Crossing the street diagonally, Joel climbed the steps and opened the bank door. A growl, then a howl of anger was followed by a pencil smacking into the wall by the door frame. He ducked, wondering if the ledger was going to follow.

"Stupid, you're just being a dunce. A ten-year-old could add up these columns better than you. I don't understand what I'm doing wrong. I get something different every time I add the stupid numbers." The gate slammed open and Tilde stomped from behind the counter. "Oh, Joel. I didn't see you come in. Did you get everything done?" She sidled sideways to the window.

"Yes, I have to gather my thoughts on the matter then I'll let you know." He watched as she squatted down, picking up the pencil that had rolled nearby. He removed his hat and coat, hanging them in the corner by the retiring room and moving next to her desk. The ledger page was crumpled, but at least it wasn't torn. "Are you finished balancing this account?"

Tilde, coming through the gate gave him an evil look. "I give up. You win. Order those stupid adding machines. I've spent more time adding columns over the past month than I should. If they will help, then they'll be worth it." She flopped down in her chair in a very unladylike manner. "Don't say it. I know I'm not sitting properly. Mother would be appalled, and I really don't care at the moment."

Joel raised an eyebrow but she didn't look at him. He went into the small supply room and brought out a large box. Setting it on her desk, he waited. It didn't take long.

"What's this?" Tilde sat up.

Joel unhooked the latch and lifted the lid of the wooden crate. "It's an adding machine. I ordered two several weeks ago. I've kept them stored away until you were ready to try one.

She stood and looked from him to the machine and back. "I don't know whether to smack you or kiss you. Ordering this thing behind my back. Not telling me it was here waiting for me to use it while I fought with the addition."

Joel pulled her to him, pressing her against his chest. "I vote for the kissing. Much more pleasant and an appropriate way of thanking me for ordering them."

Tilde reached around and spread her fingers over his back, "I'm not sure that's appropriate between the boss and the employee."

Joel kissed her nose. "Who is which?"

Tilde tapped her chin. "I'm not sure. You're the president. I'm the owner, or half owner. It's a dilemma."

"Easy enough to figure out. It's the one who gets the most pleasure from the kisses." He began giving her small, quick kisses.

"Might be hard to tell."

"We'll just have to keep it up until someone wins." His kisses inched longer and longer.

"Or someone comes into the bank."

"Maybe we should turn the sign to closed and lock the door."

"For what reason?"

Joel kissed her nose again. "Executive board meeting."

"Ah...good idea."

CHAPTER TEN

"I'M NOT SURE HOW YOU talked me into this. I don't know most of these people."

Tilde followed her mother down the stairs trying to tune out her mother's complaint. "You know Millie and the children very well, Mother. You've met Mr. Cutler a number of times at the mercantile. His children also. You've known Maude since she was a baby. This is a good opportunity to meet her new husband, Jeremiah Henderson."

"Yes, yes, I know. It's that U.S. Marshal I'm concerned about. What do they call him, The Preacher? What if he decides to pull out one of those guns and shoot us all?"

Joel, standing at the bottom of the stairs, laughed. "Nathan would never do that. I'll be surprised if he wears his guns tonight. Unless he has a Calling, he'll leave those behind at the inn."

Tonight was going to be the first time since the disaster that Lasek House was having visitors for supper.

Joel had asked that they host a gathering for Nathan Ryder who was leaving in a day or two to go back to Redemption, New Mexico where his ranch was. He wanted to get back to his family. With the situation at the silver mine taken care of it was time for him to leave Jeremiah in charge.

All the doors on the main floor were open, allowing the guests to easily mingle and Millie and Clay to keep an eye on their nine children. The dining table was extended fully with all seven leaves in place. A high chair occupied one place for Abe, Millie's 21-month-old son. Mabel hadn't been in favor of including the children until she learned that Clay Cutler was a second cousin of Nathan Ryder.

The doorbell jingled signaling the first of their guests arriving. Joel answered, admitting the newlywed Maude and Jeremiah Henderson. He was the mining engineer in charge of reopening Pike Silver Mine. A former resident of Silverpines, he'd returned to work on the mine and marry his childhood sweetheart, Maude Jones.

It wasn't long before the Cutler's arrived along with Nathan. Tilde worried that the children would act out, but they were on their best behavior, which she knew would please her 'stickler on propriety' mother.

Supper was a feast created by Dara and enjoyed by all. As the evening drew to a close, not very late because of the children, Nathan called everyone together in the parlor. He stood in front of the fireplace.

"I want to extend my thanks to Mrs. Lasek for

allowing this gathering in her home. Joel and Tilde, also. Thank you for this delightful send off." Nathan made eye contact with each of the adults. "Jeremiah, you've been reunited with your love. Blessings on you both." Nathan's polite expression changed. "All right, with the niceties to the adults out of the way, come on kids, I have something for each of you."

Nathan knelt down, opening a carpet bag next to him. "Girls, first." To each one he gave a fabric doll. "These were handmade especially for each of you by my grandmother, Penny Ryder." The girls oohed and ahhed as they accepted them. Fern led the way, thanking Nathan with a kiss on the cheek and was followed by each of the other three.

"Abe, Reuben, Ben, these horses were carved by Nugget Nate himself." Each horse was slightly different in stance. The boys dropped to the floor in a corner and began galloping them around.

"Ryder, Nathan, I've got something very special for each of you." He pulled two sheathed knives from the bag. Nathan stood and held one out to each of them. "These knives are the very ones Jim Bowie gave to Nugget Nate after he beat Jim in a fight."

Clay Cutler cleared his throat loudly. "I thought he gave that knife to me. That's what he claimed."

"Me too," Joel said.

Nathan chuckled. "He did. Nugget Nate said that to every boy he gave a knife to. We thought it was just one of his tall tales. When I first got to the ranch we went through everything. Every building, every trunk, and crate. We found several crates filled with these knives. Several more were empty. There was a letter in the open one from Jim Bowie dated before the Alamo. It said, 'Here are the knives you won for beating me in that fight. Hope this settles the bet.' The old coot was telling the truth every time he gave one away."

~~~~~

Early the next morning Joel met Jeremiah, Clay, and Nathan on the platform at the station. Nathan's Pullman car and cattle car were waiting on the side track to be hitched onto the train. Nathan bounded up the stairs with his carpetbag. His trunk was already sitting, ready to be loaded.

"Well, I didn't think I'd have a send-off this early."

"We wouldn't let you leave without a final good-bye." Jeremiah punched Nathan on the arm.

"No, I suppose not." Nathan smiled at them all. "Clay, I hear Ryder's showing evidence of having Callings."

"Yes, he is. I'm thinking Nathan might be soon too."

"Keep me posted on how they progress. If they need their heads knocked together about it any time, just send them to me."

All the men chuckled as a whistle was heard in the distance. It wasn't long before the train was at the station and Nathan's cars were hitched on.

Nathan shook hands with each man, then jumped onto the platform of his Pullman. The whistle blew as the train began its journey east.

"He's one of the last of the great lawmen of the West, isn't he?" Joel said.

"He is at that. The century is changing and the ways of the West are too." Clay patted Joel on the shoulder.

"He's one of a kind, the good kind." Jeremiah cleared his throat. "I'm gonna miss working for him."

"We'll all miss him. He brings Light wherever he goes." Clay and the others watched as the train faded from sight.

~~~~~

Tilde watched as her mother stared out the window of the parlor. Something was bothering her and Tilde didn't know what it was. It seemed as if she was accepting Joel into their family. She thought her mother had been making progress in grieving her husband and son. Now Tilde wasn't so sure.

"Mother, is something bothering you? You seem depressed."

A sigh was the response.

It was Wednesday afternoon and the bank closed at noon. After lunch Joel said he was going back to complete some work and she didn't need to come with him. Tilde approached and placed a hand gently on her mother's arm. "What is it? Can I help?"

"No, there are just so many things that have happened lately. I need to get over them, but it's difficult. I'll be fine."

"You mean the earthquakes and losing Father and

Terrance?"

"Yes, and not being able to see you married. Not planning your wedding. I know it's selfish but…" Mabel's voice trailed off.

Tilde didn't know what to say. She knew it had disappointed her mother not to have the big elaborate wedding she'd always talked about for her daughter. It couldn't be helped. Her mother's objections to Tilde placing the advertisement in the Groom's Gazette made any public wedding an impossibility.

When a tear slipped down her mother's cheek, Tilde felt more guilt than she thought possible. There wasn't really anything she could do about the disappointment her surprise marriage was. She thought she and Joel had made the right decision. Truthfully though, it was Tilde who had chosen that they marry right away without informing her mother. Now, she second guessed her choice.

Everyone in Silverpines had lost so much. Everyone was still struggling with grief and moving on with their lives. Tilde realized her mother didn't have anything to move on to. She was a widow who had lost her son. Her daughter had married without her, moving on to a new life.

There was nothing Mabel Lasek had to move on to. She kept to herself, in the house with little to look forward to each day. The activities she'd participated in before the disaster had stopped and not resumed. Ladies circle at church. Tea with friends her age. Bridge club.

Several of her friends had left town. Others were still grieving so badly they wouldn't take visitors. Several were trying to help with the businesses left to them.

In the summer and early fall, Mabel and Dara tended the garden and put up the produce for the winter. That was complete now so she had more time on her hands.

Tilde realized that her mother was lonely. Before, she only spent three days a week at the bank. Now she spent six. No wonder her mother was depressed. Not only was Tilde not around nearly as much, when she was Joel was the focus of her time. What could she do to help her mother? Tilde didn't have a clue.

"Mother, it's a beautiful day. There won't be too many more until spring. How about we go for a walk? I hear the mercantile has a new line of lace, Venetian."

"You go on, Tilde. I'll just stay here."

"Please, Mother. The bakery has put in a few tables. We could have tea there."

Mother turned and her sad eyes nearly made Tilde cry. How could she have not seen how her mother was feeling? She needed to talk with Joel about this.

First though, they needed to get out of the house for a while. Maybe they would see some of her mother's friends; Mrs. Edmondson, Miss Edie and Miss Ethel Howard. Maybe they could stop in at the bank. Tilde could show her the new adding machine. Maybe they could talk Joel into having tea with them.

"Please, Mother?"

"If it means so much to you, who am I to deny you?

Please be sure to wear your gloves, Tilde. You forgot them this morning. I found them on the foyer table." Mabel preceded her daughter out of the parlor and up the stairs to change into a walking dress. Tilde decided she'd do the same. That would make her mother happy.

~~~~~

"Okay, my dear, what's bothering you?" Joel came up behind Tilde as she looked out their bedroom window. Night had fallen and the sky was overcast so she couldn't see anything anyway. She was standing in her nightgown. The only light in the room was the lantern on his bedside table. He grasped her shoulders and turned her to face him.

"It's Mother. She's depressed and lonely. Before, I only worked three days a week. We spent much of the other days together. Now, I'm working six days." Tilde went on to tell him what her mother had told her and what she had thought herself.

"I understand. It has to be hard being alone and having dealt with so much loss."

"She just doesn't have anything to look forward to everyday. I'm the only one left and most of her social activities have stopped."

"She enjoyed your afternoon together. She spoke of seeing several of her friends while we had tea and at supper. Some of her reminisces were quite funny. I never realized she had such a sense of humor." Joel pulled her to his chest and embraced her. He hoped they could resolve this conversation and move on to a more pleasurable topic.

"She used to have, even with her focus on lady-like propriety." Unspoken were the words, 'before the disaster.'

"What do you think will help her? Would she come to the bank and help out there?"

"No, that's not something she would do. She's never worked there and doesn't have any inclination to start now." She paused, then said, "I'd like to start taking some time off during the week. Maybe an afternoon or two. Do you think that's a possibility?"

Joel thought about it for a minute, stroking her back as he did so. "I think so. Tuesday afternoon we're not that busy. Thursday morning, too. That might work better than the afternoon. The end of the month I'd like you to be there to help close out the books. Most other weeks it should work."

Tilde hugged him and jumped up, giving him a kiss on the cheek. "Thank you. I know it will make Mother so happy."

Joel chuckled and held her close. "You know what will make me so happy?"

"What?"

Joel lifted his eyebrow as he looked down into her face which lit up pink in the lamp light.

CHAPTER ELEVEN

TILDE PULLED THE LEVER ON the adding machine and smiled. She loved the thing. She still did multiple additions of a column but when she didn't get the same total she could go over the tapes and see where she punched the wrong keys. She would clip them together on the ledger page until the next month. That was the plan anyway. She'd only done it once so far when she closed the books in October.

November came in rainy with winds driving the cold into her bones as she walked to and from the bank. It kept she and her mother in the house on the days she took off.

The days she stayed home seemed to be helping her mother's attitude. There was less sadness in her eyes. Even so, Tilde knew there was a major problem and didn't know how to resolve it. Mabel was still mourning the fact that she hadn't been at the wedding. That the wedding was just the two of them and two witnesses.

And that one of those was not herself. Tilde didn't know what to do about it so she kept quiet about the issue. There really wasn't any need to bring it up since her mother dropped it into conversation at regular intervals.

"Seeing that I wasn't at the wedding."

"I missed seeing you married."

"I'd hoped you would wear my veil."

Somehow, she managed to bring her grievance up most days.

Joel had asked her how things were going the previous evening. Tilde and he were sitting on the settee by the curved windows. It was a favorite spot for them. They had turned the piece around since with winter coming they kept the draperies closed most of the time. Facing the room seemed better than facing fabric hangings.

"She seems better. At least about my spending less time at the bank. About our wedding, she's less satisfied. She knows I was the one who pushed getting married the day you arrived and without telling her. Does she ever mention it to you?"

"No, not that I recall. Can you think of anything that might help with that? Change her attitude?"

"Not unless we get married again. Have a full-blown church wedding with all the trimmings. Invite everyone in town and have a reception at the inn with a huge multi-tiered wedding cake. Then we'd have to go off on a tour of Europe honeymoon and come back in a couple of months with tales we can tell of all we'd done." Tilde sighed and laid her head on his shoulder.

"I don't see how we can leave for a couple of months. There's no one to run the bank unless she wants to." Joel began running his fingers through the hair at her temple.

"No, I suppose not."

When Joel slipped his fingers under her chin, lifting her face, she closed her eyes waiting for his kiss.

One knock sounded, and the bedroom door opened, admitting Mabel. Joel and Tilde startled apart. Joel stood stepping in front of her. Tilde felt her face heat. Drat her blushes anyway.

"Mother, what are you doing? Do you need something?" Tilde stood, stepping around Joel.

"Oh, I'm sorry. I'll go." Mabel turned around grasping at the doorknob. A paper in her hand dropped to the floor. Joel bent and picked it up.

"What's this?" Tilde took the sheet from his hand. "Oh. Are you all right, Mother? Where did you get this?"

Her mother turned slowly, a tear slipping down her face. "I was going through your father's desk. It's something I need to do." She glanced at Joel. "Your husband needs to be able to use the desk to its fullest."

Tilde studied the paper. It was a watercolor painting she had done when she was about eight. She had given it to her father on his birthday. In the picture was their house and four people. Two adults and a boy and girl.

Joel took the painting from her and used his hand to urge Tilde to go to her mother. She wrapped her arms around her and they both cried, grieving again for the loss of those they'd loved.

When Mother pulled back, she pulled a handkerchief from her sleeve and wiped her eyes and nose. "I'm so very sorry to have disturbed you. I didn't think. Your room needs to be a haven of privacy. I won't forget again. Please forgive the intrusion."

"Please don't worry over it," Joel said. He handed the painting back to her. "Keep this in a safe place. It's precious."

With a nod, she took it and closed the door gently as she left.

With the mood broken, Tilde and Joel climbed into bed. Tilde lay on her side with Joel spooned behind her. It was a long time before she was able to fall asleep.

The bank door opened bringing her thoughts back to the present. Braylon Watts came in. Tilde stood and went to the teller window. "Hello, Mr. Watts. What can I do for you today?"

"I'm here to speak to Mr. Richards. We're working on the plans for the electric junctions. He mentioned electrifying the bank. I need to know what he plans on installing electrically."

Tilde was confused. Joel hadn't mentioned anything about electricity for the bank. "Of course. He's in his office. Come right this way."

Once Mr. Watts was in Joel's office with the door closed, Tilde sat back at her desk. Why hadn't Joel told her he was contemplating bringing electricity to the bank? What for? They didn't need electricity. What could doing so possibly do to improve their work? Why had he kept it a secret? What else was he keeping from her?

Tilde tapped her pencil on the blotter. She yawned. She was tired. Her sleep had been troubled and she'd woken several times in the night worried about her mother. Now she had another thing to worry about. What was Joel keeping from her concerning the bank?

She yawned again and opened another ledger. More columns to add.

~~~~~

"Thank you for coming, Mr. Watts. I think I understand your plan. Let me know if I can help in any way." Joel opened his office door and allowed Mr. Watts to proceed him through.

The man stopped near Tilde's desk. "Your wife seems a bit tired." He grinned at Joel.

Tilde's head was lying on an open ledger, her hand on the keys of the adding machine. She was softly snoring.

Joel smiled, then sobered. "She had a restless night. I'm not surprised that she's tired. Let's leave her be. I'll see you out." Joel's voice was soft so as not to disturb his wife.

Once he'd closed the door behind Mr. Watts, Joel went to stand beside Tilde. Noticing a speck of drool on her lip, he slipped his handkerchief under her cheek. That way the ledger page wouldn't get spotted. Smiling, he went back to his office hoping no more customers came to disturb her sleep.

As he thought of Tilde's worry for her mother and the reason why, he felt bad he'd participated in causing Mabel pain. More pain on top of what she'd suffered. If he'd realized the magnitude of the suffering the residents of Silverpines had experienced, he didn't think he would have agreed to be married that first day. And without including Tilde's mother.

She wasn't the harridan Tilde had made her out to be. Yes, she was a stickler for propriety and she liked things her way. But she was mostly a grieving, lonely woman who loved her daughter and was devastated that one more thing was taken from her so suddenly. The opportunity to celebrate her daughter's wedding.

Joel remembered how much fun Mama and Annie had planning her wedding. Joel had gotten tired hearing all the details discussed every evening at supper. When he'd mentioned, complained, about it to his pa he'd been told to stop complaining and let them have their fun. It would be over real soon and not to spoil the pleasure of their plans. Mabel Lasek had been robbed of all that pleasure.

Thinking of his parents and siblings, Joel steepled his fingers and an idea came to mind. He drew a piece of stationary from the drawer and began to write.

~~~~~

"What's gotten into you, missy?" Dara scolded as Tilde set a plate down rather hard on the table. "You'll break that and herself will be that angry at you, she will."

Tilde set the next one down softly, the china barely

making a sound as it touched the table. "Joel never mentioned he was electrifying the bank. Never spoke to me about it at all. Kept me totally in the dark about it. I never would have known if Mr. Watts hadn't come to the bank to speak with him about it." She stuck her bottom lip out in a pout.

"Be careful. A little birdie will come and sit on that lip."

Dara's comment brought a smile. That was a phrase she'd scolded Tilde with when she was a child and things didn't go the way she wanted.

"He still should have discussed it with me." She began placing the silverware beside the plates.

"Maybe so, but himself is the president of the bank now. Would your father have consulted you?" Dara placed a crystal goblet near a knife.

"No, but I'm half owner now. I should know what's going on."

"Maybe so, but he's a man and not used to discussing business with a woman. 'Tisn't a man's way. Besides, you only own a quarter of the bank, if that."

"What do you mean?"

"Well, sweeting, your mother has half and with you marrying, you, at the very best, split ownership with your husband. That gives you each a quarter. Your man is the president with your mother's approval. That gives him majority say in what goes on."

Tilde stared at Dara. "That's not fair. I ran the bank by myself before Joel came."

"That be true, but you placed that ad and married him. You knew you needed help running the bank. Told me so yourself. Himself is doing so. I'm not sayin' he shouldn't have mentioned it or consulted you, but he is the president."

"It's still not fair. He should have told me," Tilde grumbled as she went back into the kitchen.

~~~~~

That evening at supper, after complimenting Dara on her ham glazed with peaches, Joel said, "Tilde knows, but I don't think you do, Mother. We are putting in electricity at the bank. There will be electric lights and ceiling fans as well as a burglar alarm that will sound loudly if it's tripped when the bank is closed." He buttered the roll he'd broken in half.

He thought of the first meal he had at Lasek House. The look of approval given to him by his new mother-in-law when he broke his bread before buttering it seemed to have gone a long way to helping her accept him. Breaking your bread was accepted as proper.

"I'd heard that the mill was generating electricity. I never thought about it at the bank."

"Mr. Watts is focusing on the downtown first. Then he plans on continuing into the residential neighborhoods. I thought it might be good to bring to the house."

"Whatever for?" Tilde's sharp tone made him look at her.

"Same thing as the bank, mostly. Lights, ceiling fans. There are electric mixers and kettles, coffee percolators.

Singer has an electric sewing machine. I even read an article about electric lights for Christmas trees."

"Do you think it's safe?" Mabel asked.

"Seems to be. They have electricity in many cities all across the country. I'm sure there will be more inventions coming that will make life easier for everyone."

"Electric lights on the Christmas tree would certainly be safer than candles." Tilde was concentrating on her meal and the words were rather grudging.

"So, shall I speak with Mr. Watts about it?" Joel could tell that Mother wanted the electricity. Her eyes were bright with interest. It was the first time she'd been so since he moved in.

Even though she was still a stickler for propriety, Tilde's mother had softened toward him. Though she was often solemn and retired to her bedroom shortly after they finished supper, his marriage to her daughter had been accepted and she seemed to enjoy his company and the lifting of burdens she'd carried since the death of her husband. He was able to do the heavier tasks needed around the house. When he'd cleared the gardens after the killing frost, Mother had expressed her gratitude by baking his favorite pecan apple pie. Dara had groused about the invasion of her kitchen but with a smile in her eyes.

Tilde, on the other hand, seemed to be more irritable as the weeks went on. She wasn't as enthusiastic about the idea of electricity in the house. It seemed another area she was hesitant to progress in.

~~~~~

"Why did you tell Mother I knew about the electricity coming to the bank? You never mentioned it to me." Tilde hung her maroon bodice and skirt in the wardrobe. She frowned. There wasn't enough room for her things and Joel's. Maybe she'd ask her mother if they could move Terrence's wardrobe in. It would crowd the room, but her clothing was being squashed and wrinkled. She didn't want to put more ironing on Dara and didn't want to do it herself.

"Pardon me?" Joel looked puzzled when she turned around. He was already in bed with a book.

"I didn't know anything about it until Mr. Watts came in and mentioned it."

"You didn't? I thought I'd told you."

Tilde clenched her teeth to keep from snapping at him. Told her about it, huh? "No. You didn't."

"Oh, I thought I did." Joel looked down at his book again.

Tilde stared at him. No 'I'm sorry. I should have discussed it with you.' No 'I'll make sure I discuss major changes and ideas with you in the future.' No, 'This is what Mr. Watts and I spoke about.' Huh, seems she was being ignored. Well, she was tired and he could just deal with her ignoring him in other ways for a few days. Maybe a week or two until he got the idea she wanted to be included in decisions at the bank.

Tilde climbed into bed, turned her back to him, pulling the covers over her shoulder and tried to go to sleep.

CHAPTER TWELVE

THE BANK DOOR OPENED AND Mr. Cliff Dermont came in. "Howdy, Mrs. Richards. I've come to make a mortgage payment," he said stepping up to the teller window.

Tilde barely kept her mouth from dropping open. Mr. Dermont hadn't made a payment since the disaster. Not that she wasn't going to accept it, but him coming in without her going to hound him, as she'd done several times, surprised her.

"Here it is." He laid the bills on the counter.

Tilde could see that it wasn't enough to cover even a month, let alone all the back months.

"It was sure nice of Mr. Richards to change the monthly amount as well as drop the late payment fees if I pay this much each month. I appreciate that. With business being so slow, it makes it hard to make ends meet and make the mortgage payments too." Mr. Dermont owned and ran the bakery. With fewer people living in Silverpines his business had suffered greatly.

"Let me get the payment book, please. I'll be right back." Tilde went into the safe and found it. She opened it and saw a note outlining the new agreement. Both Joel's and Mr. Dermont's names were signed on the page.

Another thing Joel hadn't discussed with her. She tapped the book on her leg as she walked back to the teller window.

"I'll record this and get you a receipt. Thank you for coming in today." Tilde finished and waved goodbye as the man left.

Just one more thing Joel isn't telling me. Tilde was beginning to think he was purposefully leaving her out of the decisions concerning the bank.

She went to the safe to put the book away. The drawer that held business mortgage books had fewer than she knew should be in it. Tilde pulled out the drawer with home mortgage books. That definitely had less than there should be.

When she and Joel had discussed the number of loans not being paid and those homes and businesses which had been deserted, Joel had told her he'd look into it and get back with her. Seems he'd done the first but not the second.

She stomped out of the safe intending to speak with Joel in his office. He was standing by her desk.

"Ah, there you are. I'm going to a meeting with the mayor, Clay Cutler, Marshal Sewell, and the rest of the town council. I should be back before closing. If not, I'll meet you at home."

"Joel, there's something I want to speak with you about."

He was already out from behind the counter, putting his hat on and shrugging into his coat. "It will have to wait until later. I made this appointment with him and I don't want to be late."

Tilde watched silently as he left the bank.

She wondered if she'd made a mistake in trusting him. Not that she thought he'd do anything to ruin the bank but that he'd treat her with respect as his colleague as well as his wife.

Joel was respectful enough in their private life. He had a good sense of humor and was easy to live with. He had even charmed her mother and that was difficult to do. It was at work he didn't seem to respect her and her knowledge of Silverpines and its citizens. He didn't seem to want her opinion on anything having to do with the bank.

Tilde stared at the door with her lips pursed in aggravation. It opened and Joel stuck his head in.

"I left two letters I need typed up in triplicate. I left them on your desk. Please, try to get them done before closing, will you? Thanks." He pulled his head back out and shut door.

Tilde turned and kicked her desk in frustration. Then she spent the next couple of minutes jumping on one foot and nursing her toes.

~~~~~

"For the future of Silverpines, the improvements we've been discussing are key. I know the silver mine is going to reopen and there are already trees being cut and the mill is running. With the electricity being installed, I think it's a good time to put in sewers, a water plant to pump water to all the buildings, and cobble the streets. Motorcars are becoming more popular and they work best on paved streets. Bicycles are easier to ride, too. We should put in telephones at the same time." Joel paused as he summed up the points of discussion. "In order to do this right someone needs to oversee the entire thing. The last thing we want is to have to tear out newly cobbled streets in order to put in sewer or water lines. The city planner could help with deciding how to grow the downtown. We don't want businesses starting in the residential areas."

"That all sounds very good, but who is going to oversee all that? We all have jobs. Plus, none of us have the knowhow," Luther Garrison, the town's mayor said. The other men agreed with a nod or quiet murmur.

"That's why we hire a city planner. His job will be to make the plans and layout, hire workers, manage and oversee the entire project. I know." Joel raised a hand as protests of the cost began. "Yes, it will take money. All of this will. The fees and property taxes will be what pays for all the work and supplies. They can pay the salary of the city planner too."

"There isn't enough money in the budget for any of

this," one of the council said.

"No, and there never will be. We could float municipal bond, but I don't think the citizens would vote for it. I know someone who would be able to loan the town the money and I'm sure it would be at a good interest rate."

"Who?" Luther said. "Who has that kind of money and would risk it all on a Silverpines infrastructure project?"

Joel looked at the men sitting around the table and saw Clay Cutler and Marshal Sewell smile.

"The Preacher, Nathan Ryder."

~~~~~

Joel was excited about the results of the meeting. The council had agreed to hiring a city planner and he was in charge of the applications and the initial interviews. Once he'd weeded out those unsuited for the position or downright imposters, the entire council would go over the resumes and interview who they thought were the best candidates for the job.

Taking the steps to the bank in one leap, Joel opened the door to find Tilde busy at the teller window with one other customer waiting in line. He greeted both and waved at Tilde. He'd tell her all about it once she was finished. Right now he wanted to begin writing the advertisement for a city planner that would appear in newspapers in various larger towns and cities. He hoped to have some applications by Christmas.

He set to the task and when he was satisfied with it, looked at the clock. It was an hour since he'd come into the bank. Had Tilde been busy with customers all that time? He hadn't heard or maybe noticed the bank door opening and closing. The letters he'd asked her to type had been stacked on his desk when he had gotten back, so that wasn't what she'd been doing.

The clicking sound of the adding machine handle being pulled could be heard even though his door was closed. It wasn't loud, and he'd ignored it while he was working. Why hadn't Tilde come in to greet him once she was done with her customers? She normally did when he returned from an errand or meeting. Oh well, he'd go out and tell her the good news.

Opening his door he found Tilde concentrating on the adding machine. He smiled. She really liked it now.

When she didn't look up he drew his eyebrows together, confused. Where was his happy, cheerful wife?

"Tilde?"

"Yes."

"Are you busy?"

"Yes."

"Do you have a minute to talk?"

"I need to get these ledgers balanced. It's been busy today with people making mortgage payments."

Her sniping tone surprised him. You'd think she would be happy people were finally paying on their mortgages. His talking with each business and homeowner and readjusting the payments had helped bring this about.

"Oh, okay. We can talk once you're done." He turned and went back into his office and closed the door. There was a letter addressed to him in the box on his desk. He smiled when he picked it up and recognized the handwriting. Sitting down he opened it and scanned the words. His smile grew as he read it. This would be so good.

Joel sat holding the letter thinking how much this would please Tilde. He hoped it pleased his mother-in-law too. Mabel wasn't nearly like Beulah Taylor, and Beulah had gotten so much better throughout the years but was still someone who people didn't want to cross. Mabel was mostly a grieving woman who didn't see much joy in her future. Joel wanted to give her some.

His thoughts turned to Tilde. She was so much more than he ever thought he'd be fortunate to have in a marriage of convenience. He'd known she was a beauty the first time he saw her as she stood on the platform. That she was smart, funny, and giving he learned early on. She was also stubborn, as witness to her resistance to the adding machine. Her loving it now showed she wasn't resentful of making a change.

So what was the matter today? For that matter, her attitude hadn't been as open and joyful in the past couple of weeks. Not that she was irritable or angry. It was a more subtle change. Rather than chat and tease, she was quiet, answering his questions but not really making conversation. She spoke with her mother just as normal and with Dara. It was only him she seemed to be pushing away from. And he didn't like it.

What was the matter? Was it something he'd done?

He couldn't think of anything. The bank was running smoothly. Mortgages were being paid. Accounts were being opened by the people who were moving into town. Now, with the coming improvements to Silverpines, you'd think she'd be delighted with him.

Well, nothing would come of his worry. He needed to write back so what he'd initiated could come to pass.

~~~~~

Tilde heard the door close behind Joel. She blinked several times to keep the flooding in her eyes from falling on the ledger. She was so lonely, even when she was surrounded by people. Joel didn't share things with her. Oh, he told her about things after the fact. After everything had been decided. But he didn't want her input. Wasn't interested in her ideas. Didn't even want to bounce his off her.

What kind of a marriage would they have if he made every decision without consulting her? Never wanted her opinion.

When they'd met, she'd had such hopes. He was everything she wanted in a husband. Kind, considerate, caring. He had a great sense of humor. He was compassionate with her mother, who could try a saint at times. In almost everything, Joel was perfect. Well, not perfect but pretty close.

So what was wrong? It must be her. Something about her made him not respect her intelligence. Not want to truly discuss topics and ideas with her.

A tear slipped past her vigilance and dripped onto the ledger page. She wiped it away. At least it hadn't settled on the writing. There would be no smear she'd have to explain. She doubted Joel would notice anyway.

CHAPTER THIRTEEN

"DARA, DO YOU HAVE A minute?" Joel stuck his head into the kitchen.

"For you, always. What you be a needin'?" Dara grinned at him as he came in. "A piece of pie or a cookie?"

Joel chuckled. "No, thank you. I was wondering if you had noticed anything unusual about Tilde?"

"Not off hand. Why do you ask?" Dara went back to kneading her bread dough.

"She seems, I don't know, off somehow. Quiet, reserved. Not her normal cheerful self. I was wondering if she's worried about something. If her mother is not doing as well as I think she is with her grief."

"They seem pretty normal to me. They go on outings and to visit friends on the days she's not working. I hear them laugh which is music to my ears. There wasn't any laughter in the house for too long. Herself is beginning to make plans for a Christmas party. They had one every year. I didn't think she'd want one this year."

This was the first Joel had heard about a Christmas party. God certainly worked in mysterious ways. This fit into his plans very well. Now he had the perfect reason to make his request to Mabel.

"Thank you for your time. I appreciate your help." He gave Dara a quick hug and left her shaking her head at his abrupt turn about as he headed out to find Mabel.

He found her in the parlor reading. "Hello, Mother. How are you today?" It was a Wednesday afternoon and the bank was closed. "Is Tilde around?"

"I'm just as fine as I was at lunch." Mabel smiled at him, amused. It was less than an hour since they'd been at the table together. "No, she went upstairs a while ago. Do you need her?"

Joel thought about how he needed her but didn't share that with her mother. He sat on the settee across from her. "No, just wondering. Actually, I was wondering if you could help me order something for her. I'd like to get her a dress for a Christmas present."

"Oh?"

He could tell the idea pricked her interest. "Yes, a white cashmere dress. You know, with a bodice and skirt. Something fancy in white with fur or that ribbony type stuff they sew on in loops and swirls." He waved his hands around trying to explain something he knew nothing about. There was some word his mother and sister called it.

"Gimp?" Mabel offered.

"That's it. They sew it on and swirl it around down the front of the bodice and around the skirt. It's real pretty and I think Tilde would look beautiful in something like that."

Mabel was smiling at him. "I think that's a wonderful idea for a Christmas gift. Let me get the Harper's Bazaar. It will have images we can look at. You can choose the style you like and I can send to Astoria to the dressmaker we use." She got up and went to get the periodical.

Joel breathed a sigh. Mabel would enjoy helping with this. It might not replace planning Tilde's wedding dress but it's what he could do to replace the desire.

~~~~~

Joel took a sip of coffee then set down his cup. They were just finishing dessert that evening. Supper was superb as usual. Dara was a wonderful cook. "So, Dara tells me there's a party being planned."

Tilde shot him a surprised look. "What?" She looked across the table at her mother.

Mabel smiled. "She spoiled my surprise. I've decided to hold our annual Christmas party."

"You have?" Tilde sounded shocked.

"Yes, I think Silverpines needs a celebration. We've come through a trying time and survived. What better way to celebrate than honor the birth of our Lord. I want to have an open house and a supper for our closest friends."

This was more than Joel had expected. He'd thought

there would be a dinner party for a few couples and singles who were Tilde's and Mabel's closest friends. She seemed to be wanting to have everyone in town.

"You do?" Tilde still sounded shocked.

"Yes, I do. We can decorate the house and open it to whomever wants to come that day. We'll announce it in church a few Sundays before as well as send out invitations for the supper."

"What's the date you are planning this for?" Joel asked.

"Christmas is on a Monday this year, so I thought the Saturday a week before would be good. That way it won't infringe on family celebrations but still give us time to prepare." Mabel looked at him. "You will have to let Tilde off more than two half days a week as we get closer. I'll be needing help with the planning and decorating."

"Of course. We can work around whatever you need."

"Thank you. I'm so glad. I was dreading this Christmas, but I think it will help everyone get through the holiday. It's a way I can give back to the community. Or rather we can, right Tilde?"

"Yes, of course. I'll help you plan and spread the news about it."

~~~~~

"I can't believe Mother is planning a Christmas party, and for the entire town. Well, an open house for the whole town. The supper will be smaller." Tilde sat brushing her hair as Joel picked out his clothes for the next day.

"She seems quite enthused about it. I'm glad she wants to do this. I think it will be good for her, the planning and all. She sounded so happy talking about it."

"You'll be tired of her talking about it soon enough." Tilde chuckled. "It's all she'll be interested in until it's over. Then we'll have the post mortem about how it went and how things could have been done better."

"If it makes her happy, it'll be worth it." He came over and placed his hands on her shoulders. Their eyes met in the mirror. "Will it make you happy, Tilde?"

Tilde remembered when they'd been in this same position that last night they spent in the inn. It had been such a wonderful night. She wanted that again, but wasn't sure they could get back to the same feeling. Not unless Joel began to include her in the planning and ideas of the bank more.

Joel took the brush from her hand and began brushing her hair in long, gentle strokes. Tilde closed her eyes, enjoying the sensation. When he stopped he pulled her hair to one side and bent down, kissing her neck. Tilde leaned her head to the side to give him more access. He kissed it several more times then drew her up from her seat, slipping his arms around her, kissing her on the lips.

Tilde didn't care about her irritation at him. She kissed him back as he scooped her up in his arms and carried her to their bed.

CHAPTER FOURTEEN

THE PLANS WERE GOING ALONG well. Joel could tell by the joy in Mabel's demeanor. She hummed as she wrote lists and placed orders. He only wished things were going as well with Tilde.

He'd thought they'd fixed whatever was wrong. Thought the idea of the party would bring her out of whatever had been bothering her. That night was certainly memorable. But at work the next morning she'd been as silent as ever. When he'd told her about the plans for the town and the hiring of a city planner she'd simply listened. She hadn't asked any questions, just made agreeing mumbles when he paused waiting for her input.

He was at a loss. What was he supposed to do? He couldn't think of anything he'd done that might make her shut down like she seemed to be.

Tilde certainly could hide her dissatisfaction. She was her usual bubbly self whenever customers came in. Also at church and when they met people on the street.

Joel was beginning to think something was wrong with Tilde physically. She was tired all the time. She went to bed early most nights, leaving him and Mabel in the parlor. Several times she'd fallen asleep at her desk during the day. He always let her sleep, making sure he listened for customers coming in. Some men made crude comments about him keeping her up too late at night. He cut those off quickly. He would let no man disrespect his wife.

Hearing her laugh, Joel looked out his office door. Millie Cutler was there with several of her children. Grace had that magnifying glass at her eye, as usual. Tilde handed a bank book back to Opal. Millie picked Ida up and said something. Tilde grinned and opened the gate, letting them come behind the counter.

"Mr. Richards," she said. "Miss Ida Cutler would like to open a savings account."

"I have five dollars and forty-seven cents." Ida held out her hand and the coins dropped to the floor. She squirmed to be set down and gathered up her coins before standing with a huge smile. "Will you help me?"

"Of course, Miss Cutler. I'd be delighted to." Joel noticed the frown on Opal's face. "Is there a problem, Opal?"

"I wanted you to help me when I opened my account, but you weren't here. Mrs. Richards had to help me."

"How about, once I get Ida's account open, you show me your bank book? We can see how much you've saved." That brought a smile to the pouting lips.

Joel looked up to share the moment with Tilde. The girls were so cute. She'd gone back to her desk and was punching keys on her adding machine. As he turned his attention back to the girls and their mother, he wondered again how to get back the woman he'd married.

~~~~~

Tilde opened the door to the Silverpines Apothecary and Clinic run by Dr. Hattie Childs and her husband Dr. Robert Childs. She'd made an excuse of running an errand for her mother as she'd left the house. Now she'd need to buy something at the mercantile that she might or might not need to make her excuse the truth. Well, this visit was an errand but she didn't want her mother or Joel to find out.

Tilde had worried that something was wrong with her. She was so very tired all the time. She couldn't count how many times she'd fallen asleep at her desk in the last month or so. She'd almost fallen asleep at their Thanksgiving meal. As she laid in bed last night a thought came to her. With the Christmas party coming fast she needed to know. She was at the clinic to see Dr. Hattie Childs to confirm her suspicions.

"Hi, Tilde. What brings you in here today?" Tess Daniels was sitting behind a small desk. Though both ladies grew up in Silverpines, they hadn't been in school together as Tess was somewhat older.

"Hi Tess. I'd like to see Doc Hattie. Is she available?"

"Yes, she is. I'll show you right in."

Sitting alone in the examination room, Tilde pressed her hands to her stomach. She didn't know what she was more afraid of, that she would or wouldn't be expecting. It hadn't even occurred to her that her fatigue could be caused by an interesting condition. Not until last night when she realized she'd missed her course for the last couple of months. Hence the trip to see Dr. Hattie.

The door opened admitting her. Tilde gave her a wan smile. "Hi, Doc."

"Good morning, Tilde. What can I do for you today?"

"Hum, ah…" Tilde felt herself blush and knew her cheeks were bright red.

Hattie laughed softly. "I understand. Let's chat for a few minutes then we can check you out."

Tilde left the clinic torn between joy and worry. In about seven months' time she would become a mother. One moment she was ready to jump for joy, the next she was worried about how this would affect Joel and their marriage. Would he shut her out of the decisions even more? Would he want her to quit working at the bank entirely?

"Mrs. Richards, I saw you come out of the clinic. Is anything wrong?"

Tilde nearly groaned. It was Mrs. Daniels, Tess's mother. She was also the biggest busybody there ever was. There was no way Tilde was going to let her in on her news, so she lied. "I had some bank business to speak with them about. Nothing you need to concern yourself with. Tess was there. She looks good. I haven't had a chance to chat with her much lately."

"Oh." Mrs. Daniels sounded disappointed. Bank business didn't interest her apparently. "Yes, Tess is doing well. I do wish she'd find a beau and get married though."

"Well, yes. Good-bye Mrs. Daniels. I have errands to run. Have a good day." Tilde made her escape, heading across the park to the mercantile. On the way she asked forgiveness for her lie.

When she'd purchased some tea she didn't want, Tilde wandered back to the park. She didn't want to go home or to the bank. Glancing around to see if Mrs. Daniels was still lurking behind a bush ready to pounce again, Tilde went into the park and sat on a bench made somewhat private by evergreen bushes surrounding it. The day was sunny, unusual for this time of year, with little breeze so it was comfortable for her to sit and contemplate.

Someone sat down beside her. It was Mrs. Fanny Mae Edmondson, widow of the late pastor and wonderful counsel for those who would share. Tilde leaned against her. Mrs. Edmondson put an arm around her shoulder.

"What's the matter, dear? The Good Lord told me I'd see you today. That you needed someone to talk to." She gently took Tilde's hand in hers, holding it.

Tears came and slipped down Tilde's face. "I'm so confused. Everything was going so well. We were getting to know one another and working well together. Then

Joel started keeping things from me. No, not really that. More not discussing things before he'd already made the decisions and acting upon them. Sometimes he forgets to tell me even afterwards. I ran the bank for all those months with no one to help, no one to discuss anything with. Now I feel like I'm being pushed out. I thought he wanted me as a partner, not just a teller."

"Is that what you want? To work at the bank and be a business woman?"

Tilde sighed. "I did. Now I don't know. I just know I don't want to be left out of all the decisions."

"What sort of decisions?"

"What to do about mortgages, about changes in the bank, how things are run, ideas he has about the town."

"I see. You want to have a chance to hear and contribute to the plans he's thinking up."

"Yes, that's it." Tilde sat up and wiped her eyes.

"Have you told him this?"

"No."

"Why not?"

Tilde thought about that. Why hadn't she told him, or asked him why? "I'm afraid he'll tell me it's not my business anymore since he's the president of the bank. That he doesn't think I have anything to contribute. That I shouldn't worry my pretty little head about men's concerns."

"Do you think he'll do that? That he doesn't respect your opinions?"

"No and no. It's just that he doesn't ask. Doesn't bring

me into the conversation at all. He just decides."

"Has he made any poor decisions?"

"No."

"You just want to be part of the process."

"Yes, his ideas are very good. He's going to be helping Silverpines become better than it ever was."

"So what do you think the Lord would want you to do?"

"Speak to him about it even if I'm afraid he'll tell me that it's none of my business."

"You know fear is not of the Lord."

Tilde nodded.

"You respect him, don't you?"

"Yes, of course." Tilde looked sharply at Mrs. Edmondson.

"Good, that's what the Bible tells women. Respect their husbands. It's what men need, to be respected by their wives. You show respect to him when you speak with him about this, and I think you'll find everything will work out."

She could do that. She did respect him. Respected all the decisions he'd made since they'd been married even if he hadn't included her, even if she fought them at first. And he was very good to her mother. He never pushed her to relinquish her position in the house. Never let any impatience show when her mother might see. She'd heard some of his grumbling about propriety when they were alone, but never in front of her mother. He listened when she needed to talk about what she, they, had lost.

The tightness around her heart eased. "Yes, I respect him."

"Then show him when you talk with him about how you feel. You do know how you feel don't you?" Mrs. Edmondson's slight grin told Tilde she knew how she felt.

"Yes," Tilde said softly.

"I thought as much. Well, my dear, I'll be leaving you here. I promised your mother I'd stop by. She said she had something she wanted to show me. Do you know what that might be?"

"No, ma'am, I don't."

"Whatever it is, I'm sure it's lovely. Your mother has such superb taste." Mrs. Edmondson stood, leaned over and gave Tilde a kiss on the forehead. "Take good care of yourself. It's so important during this time."

As Mrs. Edmondson walked away, Tilde reviewed their conversation trying to figure where she may have let the older woman know about her condition.

~~~~~

Joel locked the bank. He wasn't going home just yet. Tilde had taken the entire day off. It was her usual morning to stay with her mother, but she'd stopped in just before noon and said she was taking the afternoon also. Tilde looked pale and he had asked if she was feeling well. She's assured him that she was fine. She and Mabel were going to work on some details for the Christmas party. He'd decided then to make a side trip on his way home and told her he'd be late, so not to worry.

Now, Joel headed across town to the church. He hoped Pastor James would have time to talk with him. He needed advice about his relationship with Tilde. She seemed to be withdrawing more and more. She did her work but didn't tease with him anymore. Didn't have the joy she had when he first married her.

He found the pastor walking along the park in the direction of the church at the far end. "Good afternoon, Pastor. Am I interrupting anything? You seem to be concentrating." Joel fell into step with him.

"No interruption. I'm just prayer walking. I do it several times a week in different areas of town. It seems to lead me to pray for the people of that area specifically. Sometimes I get special revelation as I go along."

"Ah."

"Something I can do for you, Joel?" They were approaching the church.

"If you have a little time, I'd like to talk with you."

"Sure, come on in." Pastor James led the way into the church. There was a small room he used as an office. "What's on your mind?"

Joel sat silently for a long time. Pastor James waited patiently for him to begin. Rubbing a hand down his face, Joel began. "I'm not sure how to explain it other than I don't think Tilde is happy being married to me."

"Oh?"

"I think she was, at first. We got along well, laughed a

lot, learned about each other. Now, well, she just doesn't seem the same."

"In what ways?"

"She doesn't chat and tease with me anymore. Doesn't even make much conversation. Doesn't seem interested in the bank. No, that's not right. It's that she just does her work without comment or fussing. Whatever I ask her to do she does without complaint and that's not how we began. She fought me about the adding machine." Joel chuckled at the memory. "Now she just does the job, no comment, no rolled eyes, no heavy put upon sighs."

"Sounds like the perfect submissive wife to me." Pastor James leaned back in his chair, clasping his hands loosely in his lap.

"Huh, I always thought I wanted a submissive wife. Now that I have one there seems to be no joy in it. I want my feisty Tilde back."

"So what do you think brought about this change from feisty and joyous to submissive and unhappy? You've been married about three months, if I remember correctly."

"Just about. I'm not sure. At first she was showing me all about the bank. The mortgages and accounts and which ones were in arrears. The people who had left town, leaving their houses to the bank. Those who were still here but couldn't afford to make a payment." Joel smiled. "Then she had trouble with the sums. She got so frustrated, threw a pencil at me. Well, not at me. I just happened to come in when she threw it across the room."

Both men chuckled.

"She is feisty. I haven't been here much longer than you, a couple of month really. I don't know Tilde well, but she seems levelheaded, compassionate, caring, quite intelligent."

"She is all of those things, and more. She's really helped her mother. Mabel is grieving terribly."

Pastor James nodded. "So, when did you notice the change?"

"I suppose it was when I said we were going to put electricity in the bank. I forgot to tell her about it until supper when I was telling Mabel."

Pastor James nodded.

Joel thought about that night. Tilde had asked him why he hadn't mentioned the electricity to her. He didn't remember what he'd replied. He and Braylon Watts had everything in place for the work to start. They'd had several meetings about it.

Joel's stomach dropped. "I made the decision to put in the electricity without consulting her. I didn't include her in any of the thought process or the planning. I didn't even tell her before I told her mother." Joel wiped a hand down his face. "Then I brushed off her asking me about it that evening as we got ready for bed. That's when things really began to become chilly between us.

"I'm sure there are other times where I didn't tell her things or have her help with the planning. I can't think of them, but if I didn't notice then, I'm not going to remember now."

"Probably not."

"So, what do I do now?"

"First, pray, ask God for forgiveness for not obeying His command," Pastor James said.

"Command?"

"You know the verses in Ephesians, commands to husband and wife."

"You mean Ephesians 5:22, 'Wives, submit to your husbands?'"

Pastor James shook his head. "Why are you quoting her part?"

"What?" Joel was confused.

"Why are you quoting the part addressed to wives? That's not your command. It's only three verses. There's the next paragraph of nine verses addressed to husbands.

"*'Husbands, love your wives, as Christ loved the church and gave himself up for her, that he might sanctify her, having cleansed her by the washing of water with the word, so that he might present the church to himself in splendor, without spot or wrinkle or any such thing, that she might be holy and without blemish. In the same way husbands should love their wives as their own bodies. He who loves his wife loves himself. For no one ever hated his own flesh, but nourishes and cherishes it, just as Christ does the church, because we are members of his body. "Therefore a man shall leave his father and mother and hold fast to his wife, and the two shall become one flesh." This mystery is profound, and I am saying that it refers to Christ and the church. However, let each one of you love his wife as himself, and let the wife see that she respects her husband.'*

"It's a much higher calling. Christ gave himself up for us and husbands are to give themselves up for their wives. He's called to love her and she's only called to respect him."

Joel was dumbstruck. Sure he'd read the verses. Heard the ones to wives preached. The emphasis had always been on the submission of the women. It never really occurred to him to apply those next verses to himself.

Did Tilde respect him? She seemed to. Sure she complained when he left clothing or newspapers lying around. They'd fought over a few things in the weeks they'd been married. But she'd always treated him with respect. Never nagged at him to do anything or to stop doing something.

"Tilde's been obeying the verses addressed to her. I'm afraid I haven't been very obedient to my part."

"Without the balance of each partner obeying the verses addressed to them, one doesn't get what they need for the other," Pastor James said.

"I'm not loving her like I love myself. It's no wonder she's unhappy."

"If something doesn't change, her unhappiness may turn to bitterness, then to resentment. That woman who respects you now will stop doing so. That's when the nagging, spiteful comments will begin. At the moment she's pulling away instead of getting closer to you. Now is when you can break that by obeying those commands to husbands. Love your wife the way Christ loved the church.

"I don't mean rolling over and showing your belly, letting her walk all over you. You want her to be without spot or wrinkle. She's not perfect, just as you aren't. Just as you sometimes need to be held accountable for what you do wrong, so does she. No one likes that. It goes down easier if you feel the one admonishing you loves you more than themselves."

Joel thought about that. He'd always known how much his parents loved him even when they'd called him to task. Tilde didn't know that. They were still getting to know each other. They'd married as strangers. It was no wonder she was pulling away. She didn't know how much he loved her. Couldn't know.

Realization dawned on him. He did love her. Loved her more than he'd thought possible when they married. Loved her sense of commitment to the bank, her mother, their marriage. Loved her sense of humor. Loved when she tried to raise one eyebrow mocking his tendency to do so. Loved her responses in their intimate times at night.

"She needs to know I value her in all ways. That her contribution and ideas matter to me." Joel looked the pastor in the eye. "I've got some apologizing to do. Also, some definite things to change in how I handle things at the bank."

Pastor James nodded.

"Thank you. You've opened my eyes to some

Scripture I never considered before."

"My pleasure." The smile Pastor James gave him was sincere. "How about we spend a few minutes in prayer before you go and speak with your wife? You don't want to mess this up because you didn't ask for the right words and attitude."

Joel grinned. "Good idea."

CHAPTER FIFTEEN

TILDE SAT IN HER DRESSING chair looking out their bedroom window. She should be getting dressed for supper. Instead she was watching for Joel, thinking about her conversation with Mrs. Edmondson.

She'd stayed in the park for a while after Mrs. Edmondson left. When the cold seeped into her bones, Tilde had gone to the bank. Not that she was going to talk to Joel about the baby or the issue she felt was between them there. That was better done in the privacy of their bedroom. Besides she had more thinking to do about the entire situation.

When she was ready to leave, Joel mentioned that he would be late coming home after the bank closed. No explanation as to why or what he'd be doing, just that he'd be late. Tilde had turned away, saying thank you for letting her know, blinking away moisture that filled her eyes. Once again, he was shutting her out.

Tilde had returned home just in time for the noon

meal. Mrs. Edmondson was staying and would help as Tilde and her mother made decorations for the Christmas party. Boughs of pine trees had been brought to the house along with sprigs of holly. The three ladies spent the afternoon wiring them into wreaths and garlands, decorating them with white and red ribbons. With only a week and a half until the party it was time to prepare the house.

Over the weekend the tree would be found and cut. It was another first for Tilde and her mother as her father and brother had always done this before.

It seemed as if everything in life was divided in the before or after. Tilde would be glad when all the firsts were over. Each time another yearly event came, the grief felt by her and her mother blossomed again. It did encourage Tilde that each time seemed to be less than the previous time. Christmas would be a trying time. Her mother was putting on a good front, but she could tell her mother was feeling the loss greatly now. She wished she could do something to ease the pain. Announcing she was expecting would do so, but Tilde decided to save that for Christmas Day. It was a present she could give her mother that would bring joy back to her eyes.

She saw Joel walking toward the house. Glancing at the clock she was dismayed to find it too close to supper to start a serious conversation that might take more time than they had. As he walked up the sidewalk, Joel looked up. When he saw her in the window he smiled and waved. Her heart leapt, and she returned the gesture.

Once he disappeared onto the porch she got up and began to change her outfit.

Joel entered the room while she was still in her underpinnings. Coming to her, he pulled her against him and gave her a kiss. "I spent some time with Pastor James this afternoon. I hope you didn't worry about what I was doing. I should have told you before you left the bank."

"I wasn't worried." She smiled up at him, a teasing expression on her face. He'd apologized about not telling her. The tightness that surrounded her heart eased a little. "I wasn't worried. I knew you'd come home sometime. You wouldn't want to miss supper."

"Egads madame, you speak sacrilege. Miss a meal, never." He placed a hand on his chest as if insulted, that eyebrow high on his forehead.

Tilde batted him playfully. "You get washed and let me finish dressing. I changed into an old dress for working with the pine boughs. We made so many decorations and they are beautiful. Mrs. Edmondson stayed the afternoon and helped." She went on chattering as she dressed, allowing Joel to work the buttons up the back. She'd decided she wasn't going to hold back herself anymore. If she wanted him to share with her she needed to do the same with him.

Tilde turned to face him as soon as he finished with the buttons. They stared into each other's eyes. Joel drew her close. "Let's come up after supper. There's something I want to speak with you about."

"Okay. I'd like that." She received a quick kiss on her nose then a soft swat on her bottom.

"Head yourself downstairs. You don't want to be late for supper."

~~~~~

They excused themselves and went to their room shortly after supper. Mabel gave them a smile and waved them away. After changing into their night clothes, Tilde and Joel sat on the settee in the curve of the turret.

"Joel."

"Tilde."

They said the names simultaneously and chuckled.

"Ladies first," Joel said.

Tilde's stomach was suddenly in her throat. Now that the time was here to confess her shortcomings in dealing with her frustration. Her father had once told her never to point out the other person's faults or actions when in a disagreement. This was sort of a disagreement so she was going to keep this all about her actions and reactions. At least she hoped she could.

"Joel, I've been very unfair to you," she began.

"What? No."

She held up her hand to stop him. "Ladies first. I have been unfair. I've let something bother me and started acting in a way that shut you out. I'm sorry. I won't do so any more. At least I'll try.

"I hate how I've pulled away rather than open up with my frustration. I've kept silent instead of talking to you about it."

"What has frustrated you, Tilde?" Joel had her hands in his. The earnest concern on his face eased her fears of anger from him.

"I've felt pushed out of the bank's decisions. Felt left out of all the plans for dealing with the mortgages, the improvements, the ideas you have for the town. Like I'm just a woman working for you, not with you.

"I ran the bank alone for over five months. I did what I could to help people keep their homes and businesses and keep the bank going. Now, I feel set aside, like what I did doesn't count to keep me involved other than as a teller and secretary. It's not that your ideas and methods weren't good and right. I just wanted to be involved in your making those decisions. I don't want to find out about them from someone who comes into the bank and tells me.

"That led me to closing you out. Not sharing or relating to you. Not, I don't know, just being unhappy and a little resentful. Maybe a lot resentful.

"Anyway, I'm sorry. You've been doing a wonderful job in the bank and the community. I'm proud to call you my husband. I won't shut you out anymore."

~~~~~

"Oh, Tilde, you don't need to apologize to me. I need to do so to you. I haven't been the husband you need and want. I'm sorry. I didn't realize until today that I've neglected you. Not here at home but in the bank.

"You're right, I should have included you in my

thinking. In working out the different changes I made in the bank. You did a wonderful job those months in keeping the bank open. I know it was a struggle for you. That's why I'm here after all.

"I never meant to shut you out, to make you feel insignificant. I value your input and ideas. Not that you could tell since I was clueless as to how you were feeling.

"I won't make excuses for it. I was neglectful, and you have every right to feel frustrated and resentful. I've been enjoying the challenge of the bank and helping the town. I may have held the planning and actions close to my vest because I am enjoying that challenge. It's the first time I've had this amount of respect and responsibility. It's a heady experience. Pride is dangerous. It causes division and I certainly don't want that to be the case in our marriage."

Joel touched her face. Her beautiful wide green eyes mesmerizing him. "Tilde, I will keep you included in my thinking and planning. I'll listen to your ideas and objections. I won't take your contributions for granted. I don't want division and resentment between us. You mean too much to me to do that."

Joel leaned down and kissed her gently. "Tilde, you do mean everything to me. I never thought I could marry a stranger and end up feeling the way I do. I love you, Tilde. More than I can say."

His lips met hers. He wanted her to feel the love he had for her. Even if she never returned it to him, he would do all he could to show her his love.

Disappointment flooded when she pulled back.

"Joel." Tilde laid her hand on the one that cupped her cheek. "You spoke just what I feel. I never thought I would have the love I have for you when you stepped off that train. I love you, too, so very much."

Disappointment fled, being replaced with joy. His hand left her cheek, circling around to hold the back of her head. She allowed him to pull her against him as his lips captured hers. The love he'd tried to express to her before came back to him tenfold.

When they broke the kiss, they sat with their foreheads together simply staring into each other's eyes.

Joel stood and held out his hand. "Come. Let's celebrate what we've found."

Tilde stood, allowing him to lead them to their bed.

CHAPTER SIXTEEN

TILDE WASN'T SURE WHY, BUT she kept the news of her condition to herself. She'd stick to her plan of revealing it on Christmas. She had a feeling that Dara knew or suspected. The housekeeper knew how to keep her counsel so Tilde wasn't afraid she would let the cat out of the bag.

With one more glance in the mirror, Tilde took in her new gown for the Christmas party starting shortly. Her dress was scarlet velvet and white lace. The wide flared skirt was edged at the hem by ten inches of lace. The bodice was lace over a white satin lining on a yoke of lace covered velvet. It was finished with a high collar, flaring to frame her face. In her hair were white ostrich plumes in a velvet bow.

Joel came to the base of the stairs as she descended, his gaze met hers. She looked stunning. Tilde took his hand as she reached the bottom step.

"You look lovely, my dear. Red becomes you." As he

leaned down to kiss her, they were interrupted.

"Come, none of that now. We must be acting with decorum. Our guests will be arriving soon." Her mother's stricture came from the parlor doorway.

Joel winked at Tilde. "Is Jackson here yet?" Jackson Hershall was a young teenage orphan who did odd jobs around town. He was going to act as a butler, opening the door for guests.

"He's in the kitchen finishing his meal. I had him wrap a dish towel around his neck to protect that new white shirt I got for him." Mabel stood tall and elegant in her gown of deep blue velvet with wool appliqué covering the skirt and sides of the bodice. Sequins sparkled down the front from the high neck to the waist.

Tilde smiled as Joel took her mother's hand and softly kissed its back. "You, Mother, look marvelous. Like mother, like daughter." Pretty color came to her cheeks. Tilde realized that most likely no one had complimented her since her father died.

Extending an arm to each of the ladies, Joel said, "Let us set up our receiving line." They went into the parlor arranging themselves near the door. Tilde would be greeting the guests first, Joel next to her, then Mabel. All the doors between the parlor, sitting room, and dining room were open allowing easy passage and conversation for those attending the open house. It would be from one o'clock until five. Anyone in town or the surrounding ranches could come. The dining table was laden with small sandwiches, deviled eggs, all sorts of hors d'oeuvres, cakes, cookies, candies, tarts, along with punch and eggnog. Dara was ready to refill all the trays and bowls as soon as they were depleted.

Just as the first ring of the doorbell sounded, Jackson came running to take his place at the front door. Soon the house was filled with neighbors, friends, and new residents of Silverpines. As people came through the receiving line there were some tears as the absence of loved ones was remembered.

The Misses Ethel and Edith Howard and the orphan girls whom they were raising came with wide eyes at the elegant home and the table laden with treats.

"This is a good thing you are doing for the town, Mabel," Miss Edith said, pressing a handkerchief to her cheeks to catch a few stray tears. "So very generous to invite everyone."

"Thank you." Mabel hugged both the spinsters and sent them and the children on to the dining room.

The three Bunyan brothers came in their best flannel shirts and canvas pants. They were working at the reopened mill and logging. Big and burly, they looked in awe at the house as they were greeted.

"We ain't never been in a house this grand afore," Paul said looking around.

"I have." Peter knocked a hand into Paul's arm. "'Member that toff I was sent to with a message early on once we left Ma? His house was grander than this one. I told y'all about it."

"Oh, yeah." Paul shook Mabel's hand roughly.

"Mighty fine house ya got here, ma'am. Thanks for invitin' us."

Peter echoed his brother's sentiments. James followed along not saying anything, simply gazing around, his mouth dropped a little open.

Joel checked on Mabel to be sure she was all right. She smiled up at him. "They are a colorful set of men, aren't they?"

"Yes, they are."

"Properly appreciative though."

Tilde grinned at her mother's comment. Always so genteel, her mother. It was so good to see her mother enjoying herself. Each person who came through was greeted warmly. Several times Mabel had drawn back from the receiving line giving whoever she was speaking to a hug and a few softly spoken words. Tears as well as smiles were shared. Tilde had Jackson run and ask Dara for a stack of handkerchiefs and received a smile of gratitude from her mother.

Max and Laura Winters came from their horse ranch. They didn't stay long as they wanted to get back before night fell.

The people of the town kept coming, expressing their joy at having a social event in town. There hadn't been many in recent months. The crowd thinned as five o'clock approached. Mabel was looking tired, and Tilde hoped she could have a few moments to sit before the supper guests arrived.

As soon as the door shut as the last family left, Dara

and Jackson began removing empty trays and plates. The punch bowls were carried to the kitchen by Joel. Tilde tied an apron around her waist and began washing dishes.

"You go sit for a bit, Mother. We'll take care of this," Tilde instructed.

"I'm fine. If we all do the work it will get done faster. Then we can sit."

Transforming the dining room from a buffet to a sit-down dinner was Joel and Jackson's job. They, under strict orders not to damage the lace, removed the tablecloth and the one under the lace. Then they covered the table with clean ones.

"Why are there two tablecloths? Isn't one enough?" whispered Jackson.

"I think it's because there are holes in the lace one," Joel whispered back.

"Oh."

With the help of Mabel, the teenager and Joel arranged the centerpiece and candlesticks and set the table. Jackson scrunched his nose at all the forks and spoons set beside each plate. There was even a spoon and fork crosswise above the plate along with two stemmed glasses.

White linen napkins, folded in the shape of a swan were in a basket. Jackson, warned not to mess them up, was tasked with placing one on each plate. Well, on the plate on top of another plate.

"That's a lot of dishes to wash, ain't it?" He studied

the table taking in every plate, piece of silverware, glass, and salt cellar with a jaundiced eye. "It's gonna take me a year to get them all done."

Joel ruffled his hair with a sympathetic smile. It would be late when he and Dara finished cleaning up from the supper.

With the open house dishes all washed, dried, and put away, Dara shooed all but Jackson from the kitchen. She had a supper to prepare for eighteen people and didn't need anyone getting in her way.

Tilde, Joel, and Mabel left the housekeeper/cook to her domain and took the opportunity to rest a bit before the guests arrived.

~~~~~

Joel looked down the table from the head, seeing his wife at the foot. Seven young couples as well as Mrs. Edmondson, who sat beside Mabel, lined both sides. He stood.

"I know we welcomed you all as you arrived, but I'd like to offer another welcome to our home. It's a pleasure having you celebrate the holiday season with us. Thank you for coming and please enjoy yourselves and our repast. Pastor James, would you please say grace?" Joel sat as the pastor stood and offered thanks for the hospitality, the food, and fellowship.

Dara had outdone herself. Prime rib, baked trout, Yorkshire pudding, mashed potatoes, glazed carrots, peas, creamed succotash were passed and filled plates.

Mother Lee's rolls along with sweet butter and several flavors of jams were placed on the bread plates with appreciative comments.

Conversation was lively and joyous. Joel took the opportunity to compliment Millie and Clay Cutler about their children. All nine had come to the open house, from thirteen-year-old Ryder down to two-year-old Abe.

"The little girls looked so pretty in their matching dresses, and Fern will be a lovely young lady soon. She managed the children so well, even the older boys. When they were told they could each have a peppermint candy cane from the Christmas tree, she called them back saying they'd all get one just as they were leaving so they didn't get sticky handprints all over the place."

"Yes," said Mabel. "She was darling helping each child get a plate of food. They sat around the table in the sitting room and ate so nicely. So very polite too. They thanked us prettily as they were leaving. You are doing a wonderful job raising such proper, well-behaved children."

Joel saw Clay turn his head away from Mabel and roll his eyes. Joel smiled. He'd heard Clay talk about some of the antics the boys got into.

Though the desserts were the same as those served earlier in the day, they were arranged together on trays Jackson and Dara held, allowing each guest to make their choices.

Tilde stood when all were finished, indicating the ladies would retire to the parlor, as was customary, leaving the men in the dining room. Joel stood as well. "We men will join you now rather than take our coffee in here. We will be lighting the candles on the Christmas tree."

Soon everyone was settled in the parlor. The tree stood in front of the windows decorated with blown glass balls, stars, ribbons, and bows. Candles were clipped to many branches. Joel and several other men took long matches, lighting all the candles. Dara and Jackson stood in the doorway to see the sight.

Joel stepped in front of the tree. "I have several things to say. When I came to Silverpines I hoped to find happiness within the marriage to a stranger. I hoped to help the town recover from the events of last April. I think I've accomplished both. Well, both are ongoing and I'm hoping the future continues in the same way.

"As many of you know, the town council voted to begin rebuilding and expanding the town. With the coming of the new century, Silverpines will be installing water lines and sewers, electricity is already being installed. Telephones will soon be available. The streets will be cobbled. The ruined, abandoned buildings will be taken down. Others will either be moved to those lots or new ones built. The plan is to expand the downtown to allow for more growth. We are looking to hire a city planner to make all this possible in an organized way.

"All this takes funds. More funds than the city coffers have. I wrote to Nathan Ryder, with the council's approval, asking for a loan to make these improvements possible. His reply was negative."

A groan came from those on the council and Mayor Garrison.

"Instead, Nathan has given us more than we asked for in the loan. It is a gift to the survivors of Silverpines to rebuild our town, making it better than it was before."

Cheers rang out from the men who had groaned before, as well as all the others in the room.

When the excited chatter died down, Joel began speaking again. "With the future of Silverpines settled, I ask that Tilde come up." He held out his hand which she took as she came near. "Just like many of you men, I came as a mail-order-groom. I had only known Tilde for a few hours when we married. It wasn't the wedding she or her mother had dreamed about. Mabel wasn't even there. I'd like to rectify that."

Tilde gasped as Joel kneeled.

"Tilde, will you do me the honor of marrying me again in a full wedding, your mother walking you down the aisle in the dress she had made for you, on New Year's Eve? My parents are coming to town on the 28th if it doesn't snow too badly."

Joel was facing Tilde and her mother was sitting off to the side behind her. He could see that Mabel had her hands to her mouth, her eyes brimming with joy.

Tilde was looking down at him, shock and something else lit her face. Was that amusement?

"Joel, even though we are legally wed, you better marry me. I'm expecting and want to be doubly wed before I can't wear that wedding dress."

His mouth dropped as he jumped up. "Expecting? When? How?"

Tilde shot him an ironic look as people began cheering and her friends stood wanting to give her a hug. He wasn't going to let anyone get to her before he did. He swooped her into his arms, gazing into her face with all the love he had.

"To heck with propriety," Joel said as he captured her lips in a passionate kiss.

CHAPTER SEVENTEEN

GOD SEEMED TO APPROVE OF the wedding plans because Drew, Katie and their children arrived on time. Joel, Tilde, and Mabel, who was ecstatic about the coming ceremony, were all there to meet them. The only one of his family who hadn't come was his sister Anne, who was married with an infant.

Joel hurried across the platform, hugging each of his family members as they descended the step from the train. He hadn't been able to get much work done at the bank all morning. He kept Tilde from her work also as he kept telling her tidbits about each family member. "Welcome to Silverpines. It's so wonderful to see you all." His excitement was palpable.

He hurried them across to where Tilde and Mabel stood under the awning by the station. "Mother, I'd like you to meet my parents, Mr. and Mrs. Andrew Richards. Papa, Mama, this is Mrs. Mabel Lasek." They exchanged greetings then turned their attention to Tilde.

Pride and love shone from Joel's eyes. "And this is my lovely wife and bride, Tilde Richards." He wrapped an arm around her waist, tucking her against his side. "These rapscallions are my siblings, John, Rose, and Luke."

Tilde could see the resemblance between Joel and his father. Both were tall and lean with gray eyes and light brown hair. His father, who went by Drew, had gray sprinkled throughout his. Katie was tall with hair reminiscent of sable with amber eyes. The others, ranging in age from 18 to fourteen, were combinations of their parents. The youngest, Luke, looking the most like Joel.

"We are delighted to meet you all," Katie said. "Thank you so much for the invitation. Joel has written so much about you both that I feel as if I know you already." She hugged Tilde tightly, then Mabel.

Since the train arrived near noon, they had closed the bank leaving a sign that it would reopen at two o'clock. Once the luggage was stacked on a cart with instructions for it to be taken to the inn, they went there to enjoy lunch before the visiting Richards checked into their rooms.

Joel made sure to have Tilde sit next to him. Between the meal and dessert, he announced the plans for the wedding taking place on New Year's Eve afternoon.

Katie and Rose were excited. Luke, age 14, looked confused. "I thought you were already married."

"We are, little brother, but it wasn't what my wife

deserved. She and her mother deserve to have a full wedding with all the pomp and circumstance to go along with it."

"Oh." Luke didn't seem impressed with the idea. "That means I'll have to stay in my suit all day, doesn't it?"

~~~~~

Tilde and Mabel brought Katie and Rose into the preparations for the wedding. This gave all four women a chance to get to know each other. Tilde found Joel's mother and sister delightful, and the laughter of Katie and Mabel telling tales of their child's antics as they grew filled Lasek house whenever they were together.

Tilde was overjoyed that her mother was returning to the happy, positive person she had been before the earthquakes. She was healing and progressing through her grief. Mabel was still a stickler for propriety, but she always had been. That was just her mother.

When Tilde had revealed her interesting condition, Katie and Rose hugged her so hard she nearly couldn't breathe.

On Saturday, after they had rehearsed the wedding, the family returned to Lasek house to celebrate Christmas with exchanging gifts. When Joel opened the box from his parents he went still.

"Thank you. I forgot to pack this when I left Cottonwood." Gratitude filled his eyes as he looked at his parents, especially his mother.

Katie smiled softly at him. "I found it and knew you hadn't meant to leave it. It was rather ragged, so I mended it."

Joel lifted his gift from the box. It was a quilt mainly of green and blue squares. Sashing and cornerstones of various colors and prints surrounded four patches of green and blue.

"Katie Mama made this for me when she first came to live with us. These two," he pointed to the blue and green fabrics. "Were skirts of my birth mother's dresses. My favorite ones of hers. Mama used them to make this quilt for me to remember her and how much she loved me." He pointed to four cornerstone squares of faded pink. "She even put pink in because I was in love with that color at the time. I was three."

Tilde, sitting next to him on the settee, leaned her head on his shoulder. "How wonderful that you have it again."

"Yes, it is. It represents the love I have for both my mothers." Joel's eyes shone as he looked at the woman who had loved and raised him as her own.

~~~~~

Tilde stood at the back of the church not understanding why her stomach was fluttering with nerves. She was already married to Joel. It wasn't as if she was truly getting married. That had happened months ago. She pressed her hand to her stomach to hopefully stop the sensation. Soon her waist would swell with their child. Doc Hattie had told her it was too soon to feel the baby move so she knew it was only nervousness she felt.

"Are you ready, my dear?" Her mother's voice sounded behind her.

"Yes," Tilde said, smiling at her. "Isn't it wonderful that Joel wanted to do this for us. You and I missed out on this because of our loss. Now, we get to have one of the dreams you and I talked about over the years. Even though it's not Father walking me down the aisle, I'm so happy we are doing this." She kissed her mother's cheek.

Mabel stroked a stray lock of Tilde's hair back in place. "I am too. I'm seeing that there is a future for me now. You married a wonderful man. The coming grandchild. Moving from the master suite helped too. I didn't realize what a wonderful view you had from your room. I love sitting and looking out over Silverpines.

"I know I was against you marrying a stranger, any man really, thinking he'd take you away from me. Joel hasn't. He's helped bring me back to looking forward, living life. You did well in choosing him as your mail-order-husband."

Tilde smiled. "I did, didn't I. How about we head down the aisle so I can remarry him?"

"That's a wonderful idea."

~~~~~

The organ began the familiar song causing Joel to look up at the head of the aisle. Tilde and Mabel walked slowly up the aisle, smiles on both of their faces.

He'd wondered when he first met Mabel if she would

be a formidable, irritating mother-in-law. Wondered if he and Tilde could actually make their marriage a success while living in the same house. When he'd realized she was drowning in the depths of her grief, Joel decided to do his best to show her some of the love that she'd lost. He would never try to replace them, but he'd tried to fill in the hole left in her heart.

His focus shifted to Tilde. The attraction to her had been instant. It grew each day and it wasn't long before their marriage of convenience had become real in every sense of the word. She was beautiful in form and character. He loved her with every particle of his being. Knowing he'd caused her heartache increased his desire to be the husband described in Scripture.

The white cashmere dress fit Tilde like a glove. White gimp trailed down the bodice in swirls and loops. The cuffs of the sleeves and a wide band on the skirt echoed the design. She was absolutely beautiful.

Tilde and Mabel stood before him now. He glanced at his family sitting in the front row and back to his bride. Mabel leaned up and kissed his cheek, then placed Tilde's hand in his and stepped back, sitting down beside Mrs. Edmondson.

Pastor James began to speak. Joel must have responded correctly at the appropriate times, because suddenly the pastor was saying, "You may kiss your bride."

Joel did. More than once.

About Joel

Joel's background is mentioned several times in Wanted: Bookkeeper. If you'd like to know more about his childhood order Giving Love, book 3 in my Cottonwood Series. It's available in Kindle, KU, Print and Large Print on Amazon.

https://www.amazon.com/gp/product/B00A8P66OG/

A note from Sophie

I hope you enjoyed **Wanted: Bookkeeper**. Please take a moment to leave a review on Amazon. For independently publishing authors like myself, the reviews are extremely valuable in getting our work noticed. If you take just a few minutes you could help someone else find their next favorite book.

If you'd like to be notified of upcoming releases please sign up for my newsletter. It only comes to you when there is actual real, news about my books.

http://www.sophie-dawson.com/subscription.html

Thank you.

Sophie

Want to read more of my books? Head to my

Amazon page:
https://www.amazon.com/Sophie-Dawson/e/B0084POHB6/

Sophie Dawson is an award-winning author of Christian fiction romance both historical and contemporary. An eclectic conglomeration of interests and accomplishments, she has made up stories in her head all her life. Now she types them out. Her critically acclaimed series include Cottonwood, Stones Creek, and Love's Infestation. She's also been part of several Multi-Author projects.

Made in the USA
Coppell, TX
10 October 2025